Kuwaiti Seeker

Kuwaiti Seeker

Jim Carroll

CrossLink Publishing
Castle Rock, CO

CrossLink Publishing
558 E. Castle Pines Pkwy, Ste B4117
Castle Rock, CO 80108
www.crosslinkpublishing.com

Ordering Information:
Quantity sales. Special discounts are available on quantity purchases by corporations, associations, and others. For details, contact the "Special Sales Department" at the address above.

Kuwaiti Seeker/Carroll —1st ed.

ISBN 978-1-63357-126-6

Library of Congress Control Number: 2017955610

First edition: 10 9 8 7 6 5 4 3 2 1

Praise from Readers

This compelling story chronicles the struggles of one who loses everything including his self-respect only to triumph through his faith in God.
Tom Swift, Former Chair and Professor Emeritus,
Department of Neurology, Medical College of Georgia

Kuwaiti Seeker is a great read, journeying with the protagonist through his years of personal, moral, and spiritual struggles. Dr. Carroll insightfully delved into the complexities of Islam. It was engaging, and confirms that "if not for the grace of God," where would we be?
Dr. Doreen Hung Mar
Mission to the World Medical Associate Missionary

Kuwaiti Seeker is an insightful and exciting tale about a young Muslim man who questions the practices in Islam. The novel is a wonderful resource for Westerners who seek to understand the Muslim response to Christian outreach efforts. Spanning almost half a century, the author accurately details the events, not only in the life of the main character, but also skillfully integrates an important era in the history of Kuwait.
Dr. John Kaddis, US Physician, raised in the Middle East

Jim Carroll's extensive experiences gained from living in the Middle East, and his personal knowledge gained from working with people from all types of cultural and religious backgrounds, gives him a unique platform to tell this story of a Kuwaiti Seeker. He has crafted a dramatic picture of what happens when West meets East, Islam meets Christianity and humanity meets God. This is a riveting novel that will not only hold your interest but will teach you much about comparative religion. As an academic professor at a teaching hospital, he has perfected an ability to teach by narrative.

Rev. Michael Hearon

Interim Senior Pastor, First Presbyterian Church, Augusta

Campus Outreach National Leadership Team

Dr. Carroll draws from his rich experience as a child neurologist, both in the U.S. and in Kuwait, to tell a story of inner conflict as a young Kuwaiti searches for the truth and is found by it. The novel briskly moves to its surprising conclusion and as it does, we discover much about Islam, history, the universal human condition, and the universal need for a Savior. I heartily recommend this work.

Jerry A. Miller, Jr. MD, author of *The Burden of Being Champ: The Dropout, The Legend, and The Pediatrician.*

The characters feel real and touchable...Jim Carroll carefully weaves a web through the various complexities of life, academia, geopolitics and the inner workings of Muslim families... I found this book to be both educational, engaging and a delight to read.

Jeremy Rueggeberg, Owner and Publisher of *Behind the Fountain* Magazine and *Augusta Medical Professionals* Magazine

To my wife, Shirley, and to our Bedouin friends of Kuwait, wherever they may be. Shirley reviewed the many versions of this book, and without her, I would not have met many of our Kuwaiti friends, nor gained an appreciation of their lives.

For sin will have no dominion over you, since you are not under law but under grace. Romans 6:14.

Contents

Acknowledgements

H.R.P. Dickson's book, *The Arab of the Desert*, provided an excellent resource with its detailed descriptions of life in Kuwait from the early twentieth century. During his career in Kuwait as British political agent, Dickson immersed himself in Bedouin life. His description of the lambs and ewes as they were brought into the fold at night was biblical in character.

Wilfred Thesiger's *Arabian Sands*, perhaps more than any other travel book, captured the feel of the land and its people. I tried to translate that feel into the modern context.

Introduction

The wind of the Gospel of grace blows where it will, unimpeded into any context. Yacoub, the main character who speaks in this novel, tried to resist. This is his story.

CHAPTER 1

The Conflict Joined

S uhayb brought out the curved knife from under his dish-dasha. His only words were, "You're a thief, and I'll relieve you of your thieving hand. My Quran commands it." Where had Suhayb gotten the big, jeweled dagger? Fear soon caught up with my admiration for the weapon. Why was the Quran in the midst of our sibling conflict?

He straddled my chest. I was weak, and he was strong. Trapping my left arm under his right knee, he then grasped my right forearm with his left hand, and took the knife in his right hand. Due to the sharpness of the knife the initial pain was less than I expected, and for a moment I felt an odd relief. But then I saw blood drip from my forearm onto the sand, where the blood grew into a small pool before the sand swallowed it. The bright sunlight glistened on our wet skin, and only the slippery sweat dripping off of us prevented completion of the intended act. I slithered under Suhayb with the lubricating sweat. My forearm slid from his grasp for a moment, but he soon regained the advantage. The dust rose and adhered to our skin. By this time the other children in the schoolyard had gathered in a circle around us.

Their cry, "Suhayb is killing Yacoub," summoned the school-master, Abu Salim.

By the time Abu Salim arrived, Suhayb had transected a small artery, and the flow of blood pulsated rather than dripped. When I saw Abu Salim's frightened expression, I lost any residue of bravery and sobbed. Abu Salim seized the knife and applied pressure to the wound.

I looked up in envy at my red-maned brother, his pale skin, and blue eyes. Where did he get the blue eyes? My own dark skin and black curly hair did little to set me apart from my schoolmates at the Kuwait English School.

Abu Salim and a teacher dragged us both to the school office and forcibly set us down in chairs at opposite ends of the room. Abu Salim opened the phone line; the only phone at the school. "I must speak to Salman Al-Tamimi immediately. No, I can't wait." At least five minutes passed as we sat staring at one another. "Salman, come and get your sons. Suhayb just tried to cut off Yacoub's hand. Yacoub needs to see a doctor."

My father arrived in thirty minutes and grabbed Suhayb and me by the collars of our dishdashas. "What've you done? You've disgraced our family."

Abu Salim gave the knife to Salman, who took the weapon, examined it, and put it in his pocket.

My father dragged us to the car and gave us no opportunity to walk on our own. As the driver started the car, there was silence for several minutes.

Suhayb was the first to speak. "He took the *masbaha* [Islamic prayer beads] you gave me when I was six. I must have his hand now for my own." He was unrepentant.

In defense I said to my father, "Why didn't you give me *masbaha* when I was six?" I put my face in both hands and whimpered.

"I give gifts to whom I wish. Suhayb is the first son. You're the second."

I never wanted to see the beads again. But continuing in my mind's eye was the picture of Suhayb counting the delicately carved silver beads as he recited the ninety-nine names of Allah.

What really hurt was the fact his religious fervor exceeded my own. Why was I small not only in stature but also in belief? And how did the law of the Quran support such an attack? Was the law not designed for my best?

We proceeded to the mission hospital down by the Gulf. The young doctor prepared a glass syringe with local anesthetic, but my father interceded. "He doesn't need that. Just sew him up." So went my first encounter with Sharia law, and my blood had counted for nothing.

* * *

We arrived home in Bneid Al Qar late in the afternoon, and our mother, Fatima, met us at the door with a questioning expression. She saw the bandage on my forearm. My father explained, "He's a thief. He should have lost his hand." My mother was not free to argue with Salman, and she kept silent as the details of the day came out in pieces.

Suhayb recited his side of the story. "He took my father's gift to me." There was no excuse. It was true.

I was sorry for my mother, who may have felt responsible for me. She was partial to me in defense of Salman's preference for Suhayb, but I had failed her again.

The events of the day were only a continuation of an ongoing battle between Suhayb and me. Had we forced our parents to take sides?

The evening closed with a typical event. Fatima laughed at my latest game. I donned a toy stuffed camel on my head in imitation of Suhyab's red mane and chased our laughing cousins around the courtyard, growling in make-believe anger. "I'm a big, red lion, and I'm going to eat you."

The next day we had to return to school and face the questions.

CHAPTER 2

School of Torture

Both of us should have been dismissed from the school. Fighting was not allowed, and certainly not with a dagger. My father assured us he had secured our continued attendance despite our disgrace. "They're taking you back only because they have no choice. I'm rich with many sheep and goats, and now there is the oil. The Emir lets us have a little, and even with the leftover oil, we could buy the school. Both of you must thank me for making your life too easy. You don't have to live in a tent as your mother and I did."

Suhayb walked into the school with his head high, as if he was proud of his attack.

I hung my head. I was unwell again, as I was on so many school days. I was too small for my age, and I often fell asleep in class. But my teachers indulged me.

School was painful every day, and the day of my return after the attack was no different. The classwork demanded endless repetition—word recognition, multiplication tables, boring facts of all kinds—the whole class repeating them over and over in unison. It was a song of prolonged torture. But if there were questions, I always had the answer. My teachers couldn't challenge my knowledge even though I slept through their teaching.

Zahra, the anxious little girl sitting in front of me, was asked to repeat the times table for sevens. She was afraid of making a mistake, and she stumbled at seven times eight. She was rewarded with a sharp rap on her hand with a wooden ruler. Crying in response to punishment was not allowed. Such was the treatment of those who failed at rote memorization.

To occupy my mind, I concocted stories. As our desert predecessors had collected around the fire for a tale, my classmates gathered around me on the playground for the narration of a story. My gifts lay in stories, and the day of my return from the embarrassing attack was no different. I began, "There once was a camel who knew what was going to happen in the future. The camel was white. The white camel belonged to me, or perhaps I belonged to him. I tried to keep the camel from coming to me in the morning of my dreams, but the camel would not obey. I think he was a good camel, but he wouldn't mind me. Sometimes I wish the camel would just go away, because the camel told me things I didn't want to know. Is this a betrayal or a trick? The camel told me my brother was to hurt me, and the next day my brother attacked me with a knife." Those listening had witnessed the attack, and they looked at each other. "The camel told me my father would not love me like my brother. He told me only my mother loves me." Even then, the white camel could be cruel.

"But the scariest part is that the camel told me I would search for something I wouldn't find on my own. And that something would be the most important thing in my life. I tried to make the camel go away, but he always comes back. He tells me I'm going to be famous and that he will give me more stories to tell. I think the white camel follows me." Some of the children looked around for the camel.

One asked, "What is the most important thing?" I had no answer. I was not certain if anything about the story, or the camel, was real. But the camel had announced his presence, real, either in truth or dream. Yes, he was charming, but I couldn't be sure of his character.

* * *

I hoped none of the children would tell Suhayb of the story, because I knew my father would then be informed. But Salman did learn of the story, and I hid in my room while I heard the argument. Salman said to Fatima, "Who has been in my house?" Was this an accusation? "Who is this pedantic little maker of stories who lives in my tent?" I learned another new word from my father: "pedantic." I wanted to tell my father that my love of words had come from him.

But there was no room for such talk with my father. He was preoccupied with his search for more grazing land to replace what the Emir had appropriated for oil drilling. He was often absent, trying to repair the damage to his flocks. Suhayb was asked to accompany Salman while I remained in the walled family courtyard.

I learned to escape the slow torture of primary school and life in the Al-Tamimi household. I lost myself in my own thoughts. The white camel became more and more real, and after a while the white camel was always there in my morning dreams. Once, the camel laughed, if a camel can laugh, as he departed my bed.

While the stories preserved my position among my classmates and teachers, my moodiness and frequent episodes of spontaneous daytime sleep made me an object of ridicule at the most inconvenient times. My school classes were often interrupted by the shout, "Look, the storyteller is sleeping again."

The sleep plagued by morning dreams left me anxious, because I suspected there might be truth concealed in what was usually, and should be, obscure. My abiding anxiety made me seem strange to my peers, causing them to avoid me much of the time. But at the same time it was a relief to be avoided. My early morning events often prevented me from attending school, and while the dreaded morning visions often frightened me and left me too anxious to get ready for school, they had that small dividend.

There was a recurring theme in my dreams. Their eccentricity alone was such that I did not wish to report the dreams, even to my mother. The white camel, the central character of my dreams, seemed rather unlike an animal, but more like a character in a play. His personality—I was certain it was a male camel—was confident and aloof, except for the occasions when he teased me.

I awoke in my room on the morning of Monday, December 4, 1950. I was twelve. I was lying on my back, and although awake, I couldn't speak or move. I had been dreaming of the white camel, who was stealing sheep from my father's flock. I tried to prevent the theft, but the white camel laughed at me and proceeded off across the desert with the sheep. Mama came into my bedroom and found me looking up at the ceiling, drenched with sweat, un-speaking and without movement. I couldn't respond to my moth-er's anger about my failure to rise for school. "Get up, Yacoub. Don't give your father any more excuses to blame you." After what seemed like hours but was actually only a few moments, I regained the ability to move.

I tried to explain to my mother what had happened, but she was unsympathetic and even threatened to inform my father. I didn't want to tell my mother this event she had just witnessed was a common occurrence, and I modified the explanation to minimize the event. "Mama, my stomach hurt too much to move."

After seeing Fatima's reaction to this event, disbelief and all, I learned to keep these occurrences secret. As I approached ado-lescence, I saw this as just another indication that I was peculiar. Stories were my refuge.

CHAPTER 3

Out of My Element

The days on the desert in the spring, beautiful with the rise of the green shoots of gras, and beloved by the rest of my family, because they told themselves they were returning to their nomadic roots, were an awful time for me. As was the custom, the tribes, which had formerly come from the desert, took the occasion to return in the early spring. The temperature was moderate, and the black tents were livable again for those who had resided in the city.

But for me, the nights in the tent placed me too close to the rest of my family, and even to the herders employed by my father. I couldn't conceal my distaste for the desert life, and I had no idea what to do with the animals. And there were the morning events I often experienced, easy to conceal in my own bedroom, but not so when sleeping near others. In the desert my place at night was next to Suhayb, who wasted no opportunity to vex me.

Suhayb was in his element, and he pleased our father with his skill in camel riding, navigating the desert, and in reading the directions from the stars. Suhayb had even bothered to read a book on travel by celestial means. "Papa, I see the star that can guide us." He pointed to the North Star. On the other hand, I saw the stars only as a lovely jumble, an object for questions and wonder, rather than a heavenly map.

While Suhayb loved the time with animals of the herds and their herders, the camels, sheep and goats, I couldn't understand their ways, and the strange skills of the herders puzzled me.

The lambs were brought in first to the tent area in the evening, and each was tethered separately. Perhaps an hour later in the dark night, the ewes were brought in. Nasser, the chief herder, then called out the name of each ewe, and as the ewes came up to the lambs, he matched ewe and offspring without fail, even in the night. Nasser told me he knew the animals individually, not only by name, but also by feel and odor. I thought it an unnatural skill.

It was only then that the recollection of the schoolyard fight and the knife came back to me. Nasser was from Yemen and there in his belt I saw the traditional Yemeni dagger, or jambia. The large red jewel affixed to the bone handle was unmistakable. Nasser was the source of Suhayb's weapon. Was I so out of step with my surroundings that even the herdsman was a threat? Why would he give his precious jambia to Suhaby to punish me? My concern was compounded by Salman's return of the knife to the Yemeni herdsman. What was my place in this family? And what of the law of the Quran that motivated Suhayb? What more should I learn about such a law?

But it was the incident of the dhub that finished me for these spring forays into the desert. Suhayb proposed the venture. "Father, I saw a lot of dhubs over on the other side of the dunes by the water hole."

I had nothing but fear for the spiny-tailed lizard, often nearly a meter in length. The animal was so quick I could not see how it would be possible to interrupt its dash to its burrow. Would the dhub's sharp spines reward me with serious wounds if I actually caught one? I saw the only real reward to be a tasty grilling over the fire, and someone else could just as well achieve that prize.

Suhayb said to the men in the tent, "If we go out this evening, I'm certain we can catch several for breakfast. I bet I can catch more than anyone." I had no doubt he could do so.

Salman agreed, "We'll see who has courage to catch them." Salman seemed to know this event would be favorable for Suhayb and painful for me. Fatima kept silent, as there was no way for her to rescue me.

I couldn't refuse the silly endeavor. I already saw Suhayb capture and torture one of the poor dhubs during the day, and I did not wish to repeat the matter at night.

Perhaps the dhubs would not appear. But, no, there they were. The moon was bright, illuminating the desert, and there was no excuse. Suhayb was the first to make a capture. Salman gave congratulations while Suhayb cut off the animal's head and deposited the carcass in his basket. Another and then another became Suhayb's victim.

I knew I had to get one, even if the beast stabbed me with his spines. "There's one. This one's mine." My father laughed at my clumsy efforts.

As I was about to complete the capture, it happened. I lost strength in my trunk and legs, and I fell face first into the dune as if I were a wet rag. I couldn't move or speak. Suhayb was on the dhub and completed the capture, all the while enjoying my failure. "He's fainted. The great dhub has frightened him to death." But I had not fainted. I was unable to move but fully awake and able to hear Salman's derision. Of course there had been similar episodes upon awakening in the morning, but never before when I was up and about. The event itself, which I did not understand, frightened me, and made me think there was something seriously wrong. But in the face of the men's taunts, I could not reveal concern about the event. Was there some magical significance, or was I ill?

The spring foray into the desert that year concluded with a two-day trip by the men on camelback northward to the border with Iraq, formed in that area by the Wadi Al Batin, a rocky rivulet. Salman organized the trip for Suhayb so he would not forget his Bedouin roots. The trip was painful for me. The camel saddle was agonizing and unpleasant. As we reached the wadi, I saw low-lying rock cliffs surrounding it. Had the little stream once been a great river? The wadi still contained gently flowing, clear water from the spring rains, and we dismounted. The others washed and drank. I stood by my camel. Salman, Suhayb and the other men gloried in the scene but I vowed not to repeat such a journey.

CHAPTER 4

June 1956, King's College

S uhayb outmatched me in nearly every aspect of Kuwaiti life, and I could only lean on my academic success and storytelling.

But the time for my distinctive abilities approached, and my father let it be known that my academic prowess qualified me for university in the West. I was thankful he took this occasion to be proud of me.

When June 1956 arrived, at the age of eighteen, I prepared to depart for London. Salman made ready for my exit with re-newed vigor and apparent anticipation. My bookish ways made me stand out as unmanly, and he was eager for me to go.

Father accompanied me to the Al-Nughra airport outside Ku-wait City, and neither of us spoke during the car ride. I boarded the newly created Kuwait Airways flight to London, which was a by-product of the now-flourishing Kuwait Oil Company. Our parting was a formal affair, and the emotional elements were stiff and unyielding.

"Good-bye, my father, I love you."

"Good-bye, my son. May the peace of Allah go with you."

The farewells were completed with a loose embrace, and I boarded the DC-3. Fatima was not expected to be there, though she was losing her favorite son.

* * *

The world I entered when I stepped off the plane was one for which I was not prepared. While my knowledge of English was sufficient for admission, it was not adequate for the level of communication I desired. I was accustomed to being shielded from interaction with unrelated women and now they were all around, not regarding my presence, dressed indecently, speaking openly, hair uncovered. A young woman with long blond hair jostled me as she rushed by, and the contact jarred me.

My father arranged for Ali, who had lived in London for several years, to meet me. I couldn't have survived otherwise, and for a brief moment I mentally thanked my father. Ali cautioned, "Don't look at the women. You'll be tempted, and they will look back."

Then it was off to the university at the Strand campus on the Thames where I was introduced to my Welsh roommate who had initiated his own arrival with a drunken debauch the prior evening. The juxtaposition of my own ideas of propriety and those encountered were too much for me. I promptly fell into the middle of our dorm room, subject to one of episodes that appeared to be a fainting spell, but really consisted of loss of body tone with preserved consciousness. My roommate, Adam, saw this as hilarious, and it was not a favorable introduction. "You're drunker than I am," was his opening greeting.

By morning, however, Adam had recovered his sobriety, and we made our temperate acquaintance. "Yacoub, I'm completely embarrassed. I've never been on my own before. My father would be furious." His father was an Anglican minister from Wales. Adam's own introduction to London and King's College had been his visitation to the pubs of London in the nearby Covent Garden neighborhood. He continued, "I'm afraid I disgraced myself last night. The freedom was too much for me."

It was on this honest basis that our continued friendship began.

We both faced contrasts to our prior lives. Adam, with his religious upbringing, and I, with my displacement from the certainty of Islam, looked together at how we would integrate with our surroundings.

The timing was propitious. One June 5, during a Milton Berle variety show, Elvis Presley introduced "Hound Dog" into the medium of evening television. I had not seen television previously, and never had I seen such a vulgar performance.

Why would one keep a dog, a creature considered filthy to me as an Arab? And what did Presley's hip movements, movements that should only occur between man and wife, have to do with the dog? I could only speculate.

One June 23, I picked up the *London Times*. On the other side of the world near Kuwait, Gamel Abdul Nasser was elected president of Egypt. Nasser dreamed of Arab unity and hoped to coalesce the spirit of the Arab people in a way that had not come about for 1000 years. I had read earlier of Nasser's narcissistic views. As all former and subsequent Arab statists, Nasser viewed himself as the next Saladin, the honorable foe of Richard the Lionhearted during the third crusade. I understood Nasser. Such were the contrasts into which I proceeded.

The world I found outside Kuwait was baffling as the variety of courses open to me was puzzling. I had not previously been offered choices. I thumbed through the pages of the course catalog wondering at the immense variety of topics and disciplines.

Only my gift for languages preserved my marks. My English had been unparalleled among the students in Kuwait, but now excellence in English was the norm. Moreover, the lack of requirement for rote memorization left a vacuum in my study schedule, which I could now devote to thoughts and speculations rather than the words of others.

I altered my dress so as not to draw attention to myself. Adam was irreplaceable in this endeavor. He commented, "You can't keep wearing that robe and the cloth on your head. This is London." Only with these new clothes could I be comfortable in the pubs the King's College students frequented. The dishdasha, gutra and iqal were put aside.

The taste of ale was new. But if I went to the pubs, there were no other choices if I was to participate in the social milieu. I didn't at first care for the warm, slightly bitter flavor, but I soon learned to enjoy the liberating effects of the alcohol.

The young women were a puzzle. I had never experienced interaction with women outside my family. For some months their direct eye contact frightened me and caused me to seek refuge. But I discovered the women were seeking my company and stories. "Please, tell us again about riding a camel in the desert. You're like someone from a travel book." I complied but did not enjoy that particular identification.

The years at King's College passed quickly and I was no longer a young man in a dishdasha from the desert. I had assumed the dress and demeanor of the London college student. My facility with language paved the way for these departures. The pubs of east London were now comfortable as were the direct gazes of the young women. My dark features with delicate but sharp angles were unusual enough that I had no trouble attracting their attention. What was the point of struggling against this advantage? What would have been a crime against Islam in Kuwait became commonplace for me.

Molly's red, free hair had intrigued me from the beginning. She displayed herself to me in a manner completely routine for her, but nonetheless striking. I first spoke with her on Wednesday evening in the Red Lion. "Why are you looking at me with such intensity?"

"Because I want to. Is that a problem for you?"

On Friday we spent the night together in her flat. This was a first for me, not so for Molly. There were days when we didn't go outside. My schoolwork might have suffered except for the fact that I had mastered the requirements of my courses to a high degree. My writing skills preserved my marks.

Then, there was Audry, again at the Red Lion. There was overlap between Molly and Audry. I tried to decide if I felt guilty about the double-dealing. I couldn't decide, so I proceeded with the duplicity. I consumed more and more of the warm brown ale to obscure my thoughts of concern about the behavior.

After all, if I were back in Kuwait, I would have two wives like Suhayb, and Islam prevents me from wedding these two unbelievers. Weren't they like the captured slave concubines of my desert ancestors?

The split between my father and me had widened. Salman informed me I should acquire skills in business and return to Kuwait in the burgeoning petroleum business. But I majored in history, thus departing from my family's objectives.

I avoided returning to Kuwait my last summer in London. During the month of August, I made my rounds between Molly and Audry, and then finally with my newest addition, Anna. *Perhaps if there had been more time with Anna . . .*

When I boarded the plane for New York, I was drained of all my physical resources. My eyes fell shut as soon as the plane reached cruising altitude.

I had been accepted into the PhD program at the University of Arizona in Tucson, and my professor had agreed to my chosen area of research: the history of Islamic law, or Sharia. The idea of a lawbreaker studying the law appealed to my sense of irony.

I had taken five years to complete my degree at King's College. Most importantly, the extra courses allowed me to extend my time away from the conflicts in Kuwait.

It was August 1961, and the newspaper headline read, "Israel's first nuclear reactor is active." The Gulf States were fuming.

Thanks be to Allah I did not return to Kuwait and my father.

CHAPTER 5

Another Desert

The New York skyline whacked me in the face as the plane landed at Idlewild Airport. How would my ideas and beliefs fit in with all this?

Given my facility with language, near absence of accent, and Western dress, I had little trouble with immigration, and I boarded my flight across the US to Tucson. Soon I was back in the desert, not quite the desert of Kuwait but, except for the Sagauro cactus, very close.

I left my bags in my room on campus and went over to the Arts and Sciences Building to meet my professor, Dr. Saturnalia Allison. She was much younger than expected, surprisingly so for a full professor. I had not known her first name, and I briefly wondered if her parents had given her the name or if she had chosen it herself. She had short brown hair, horn-rimmed glasses, and wasn't wearing her shoes. Her blouse was unbuttoned down to the third button. Perhaps she was just not careful about her appearance.

"Well Mr. Al-Tamimi, you must be quite tired from your long trip. I'm glad you came over for a few minutes. Here's your curriculum for the semester." She handed me a three-inch stack of assignments. Apparently, she was more careful about scholarship than her appearance.

She launched in, leaving no space for my response. "So you're going to study Sharia, eh? I don't know anything about Islamic law, except it's a mess. But I'm sure you'll straighten it out for me. You'd better."

Dr. Allison, although a declared agnostic, was a recognized expert in Islam, and in particular, the history of Islamic law. What could I teach her? Perhaps she was open to a good story.

Once back in the dorm, I took a deep breath, lay down on the bed and read the mail that had arrived in advance of my arrival. There was an interesting letter from Anna. She had missed a period.

There was a letter from my mother, longer than I had ever seen from her:

> My Dear Boy Yacoub,
>
> Your clever little niece is writing this for me. She is very sweet to me now that I am an old woman.
>
> I am sure you are happy in your studies and that they are sufficient for your contentment. Your long absence has hurt me a great deal, and I don't know if I shall ever recover from it. Your father and Suhayb have put me aside from their lives, as I expected they would. The other young ones do not replace you.
>
> There is much news. Your father is enamored with oil, and he is making a lot of money. I do not see it. He has taken another wife. She is young, and she does not obey me. Our house is one of constant turmoil, and your father sides with her. He makes his bed with her. She is from a tribe lower than ours, the Mutair, and her habits are coarse. You know they breed horses and camels. Her way of speaking reflects her base experiences, and she does not respect me as the older wife. Most of your father's friends have kept one wife,

but not your father. Can you put this right when you return?

Suhayb is more than I would have expected. He is not soft and full of stories like you. You know he is strong, but now he is stronger than I would have known. He leads the family. In many ways he has shouldered aside your father. When the men pray, he leads. Can you believe this? He talks with the imam as an equal. I don't know how you can contend with him. You must prepare for him.

I hope I live to see you return.

My love to my son,

Fatima

I intended to write a response but it would require more effort than I had left. I needed a source of rejuvenation.

I opened my Quran, which was the beginning of my research into Sharia, and now over a matter of immediate importance. I was confused over status of abortion—was it murder? First, the Quran. I turned to 17.31, which seemed clear, "And do not kill your children, surely to kill them is great wrong."

Then I located the hadith that says life is not breathed into the child until 120 days. So perhaps the 120 days was a time of freedom. My heart strained my intellect, but I proceeded with the necessary:

Dear Adam,

It is difficult for me to contact you in this matter. I am sure you remember Anna from the Red Lion. As you are aware I stayed with her before I left for the US. We separated sadly but both of us had other business.

She has written me now she is pregnant. I am sure the baby is mine, and she writes, too, she is sure of the same. She only stated this as a fact. She did not ask anything of me, nor did she inform me of her plan. She is a brave girl and would not ask for help.

So, I must ask for your help in this. I am embarrassed to bring you into this but I feel I have no other choice. I know you know many people in London, someone who could handle this sort of thing, a doctor who is able and willing to do what is practical. Let me know the cost, and I will wire the money.

As you have been to her apartment with me on several occasions, you are able to reach her. Please go to her with the necessary information as to where to proceed and give her the funds for the procedure. It is important this occur before she is more than four months along.

Please know that I have not responded to her letter and will not do so. For my family, I want to stay out of it. I'm afraid your opinion of me will be fractured even further by my seeming coldness, but I want to put this behind me.

If you can take care of this, I will be forever grateful.

As Ever,

Yacoub

I read the letter over. I was upset by its tone. I was appalled at how cruel I now perceived myself. I started with the Quran, and I had devolved to this. Was there any absolute knowledge in this matter? I found support for the plan in my study of the hadith versus the Quran. Is this where my doctoral thesis was headed?

I sealed the letter and headed off to the post. Returning to the dorm I caught sight of Dr. Allison as she was speeding away from the faculty lot in her Alfa Romeo. She was driving too fast. My mind wandered, allowing a brief relief from the Anna episode.

Back in the dorm I went again to the Quran. I wanted to know what was right, as least for the evening. Was it the mathematics of the issue that failed or the law itself?

And now there was the letter to Fatima:

My Dear Mother,

Perhaps my little niece can assist you with this letter.

I am sorry to hear about the troubles you are having there with father and Suhayb. I will try to help when I return for a visit, but I cannot come until after this school year.

You would be proud of me if you could see me now. I have completely altered my appearance and speech such that I might be mistaken for an American. My marks for the year from King's College were the highest among the history majors.

I made many friends in London who will be forever close with me, much more so than my peers in Kuwait.

Please do not worry about me here. I have found my professor here to be very helpful, and while she could never replace you, she is very motherly. You would consider her a kindred spirit.

I am looking forward to my return next year.

Much Love,

Yacoub

I re-read the letter searching for elements of truth. There were few.

CHAPTER 6

Lost in Lust and Dreams

I was alone, it was morning, and I was unable to move. My dream, or hallucination, was of Dr. Allison, who taunted me with her careless demeanor and dress. I was able to prolong the usually brief paralysis. Then, after the enjoyment, I was late for my meeting with her.

Her office was cluttered with paper piles about the floor. "Are you not yet adapted to the time change, Yacoub?" She was initially forgiving but she turned on me. "My time is valuable, and yours is not. Don't be late for our meetings again, under any circumstances. Because you're late, I will not chat with you today, and you must listen carefully to what I will say. There will be no exchange."

Even though I had been in the West for more than five years, I had not experienced a woman taking control of the situation in such a forceful and intimidating manner. I didn't like it. Of course, she didn't know I had been with her already this morning.

"I've written a paper that's going to be published. It deals with the area you're going to take on. So, I want you to take the paper, keep it to yourself since it's still not yet in press, read it tonight, write up your comments, and return them to me tomorrow morning. You may go now." She turned back to her desk.

I took the paper and got up to leave.

"Please close the door behind you."

Already a full day faced me with several new classes, but it was no time for excuses.

In the evening I settled in my room to read her paper. It was highly technical and dealt with many areas with which I was not yet familiar. Her topic was the Hanbali School of Sharia, or Islamic Law, which at least I recognized as the major line of thought in Saudi Arabia. I had been taught it was extremely conservative. Her thesis, however, was that Ahmad ibn Hanbal had traveled about indiscriminately collecting hadiths from many sources and then crafting his own ideas into law. This idea was offensive. The idea of holy law being constructed by the view of one man, however brilliant he was, was ridiculous, and my critique of her paper reflected this. In the morning I dropped off the material and went to class.

Midday, Professor Allison spotted me on campus and summoned me. She employed an upright motion of the fingers of her extended hand, palm up. In the Arab world, such a hand motion would be deemed vulgar. Did she know this? The proper Arab mannerism was similar but with the fingers and palm pointed down, the critical difference. We talked under a tree to escape the desert sun.

"Yacoub, I'm disappointed in your write-up. I think I may have made a mistake accepting you into my program. What you wrote was immature. I can only say you have a great deal of work to do. We shall have to spend time working this simpleton streak out of your mind. I'm afraid you're stranded in *fiqh*." I didn't grasp the full meaning of the Arabic word. "Get settled in, get your mind down to the real world, and we'll talk again."

I looked at her, and she looked at me for a moment. Academic reproach was unfamiliar to me, and I had no response. Was my critique too severe? I failed to apprehend the point of her little tirade.

Why I was so upset? Was it the fact I found the professor attractive despite or because of her roughness? Was it a deeper matter? Was it the content of the paper that questioned the authority of Islam? I grappled with the difference between fact and belief, but I saw no way to breach the chasm. The ongoing ambiguities in my mind caused me even to question the importance of this dichotomy.

Or perhaps I was stuck in *fiqh*, which I didn't understand.

Before I had arrived in Tucson, one of the courses I signed up for was Dr. Allison's, The Historical Method of Ibn Khaldun. Now I would have to face her on a regular basis. I would have to redeem myself.

Ibn Khaldun captivated me. I managed to get through the *Muqadimmah* quickly in Arabic, which was a definite advantage. *So an Arab wrote this.* I underestimated my fellow Arabs. Now I saw why Toynbee hailed this work as the pinnacle of historiography.

For my class research paper I chose Ibn Khaldun's view of economic development, which is the essence of conservative economic policy.

A month passed and the three other students in the class had been asked to deliver their papers. Then Professor Allison asked me to come to her home one evening to discuss the project. Had the other students been asked to come before me?

When I arrived at the one-story Spanish style home, no others were present, and she was dressed in sweat pants and shirt with no shoes.

I took off my shoes at the door and put them in the pile. The yard was full of sand, and Dr. Allison made it clear she wanted none of the desert in her home.

"Please come in and relax. I'm anxious to hear about your paper. I hope you didn't take Khaldun too seriously. He is completely *fiqh* in his approach, as I am sure you noted." She used the word in the derogatory sense. *Fiqh*, as I had learned, in its general meaning has to do with Islamic jurisprudence, but more specifically with the law derived from Quranic principles, and not from the Quran itself. Therefore, to my great concern, the use of the word implied that an idea is not from Allah himself, but rather a product of human reasoning. The word struck a dissonant note, which subverted my desire to know what Allah intended. Her use of the word in regard to a piece of literature I thought highly of challenged my remaining sense of certainty.

"Dr. Allison, thanks for taking the time for me."

"We have plenty of time. My husband is away, as usual." She sat down on the couch nearby and pushed her hair back.

"How would you like me to begin?" The situation of being alone with the professor in such a relaxed atmosphere caused tightness in my chest, and my facial expression must have been strained. She was making me uncomfortable, and she appeared to enjoy it.

She popped up from the couch, poured us both a glass of red wine, and without asking if I wanted it, gave me the glass.

"Do you understand what you've read?"

"Yes, I believe I do."

"Do you understand how the work relates to your Quran?'

"Well, it's not from the Quran."

"What's its relation to the Quran?"

"I don't know how to answer that."

"What distinguishes the Quran?"

"The Quran is from Allah."

"Is there any other word of any type that we know from Allah?"

"Of course not." I gave the Islamic answer expected of me.

"So you see my point. What then, is the value of *Muqadimmah*?"

"It's a brilliant work."

"But it's the work of a man."

"Yes, but..."

"You know the word *fiqh* I've already used. Why would I use it in respect to Khaldun's work?"

"Only if you are calling everything *fiqh* that's not Quran."

"Exactly," said Professor Allison. "That's precisely why I told you my husband isn't here. You're a quick young man. You should be getting my drift. Here, only here, you must call me Sattie. Are you familiar with the long form of my name, Saturnalia?"

"I think it's Roman."

"Look it up. Tonight we'll have the Feast of the Saturnalia. So, this is a night of *Fiqh*, which we've already found to be outside your Quran."

"Does this *fiqh* have any boundary?"

"How could there be a boundary if it is not revealed?"

"What about my paper?"

"I've already given you an 'A.'"

The evening from its beginning to this point was not at all as I had anticipated. I did not expect to have any control over the course of the visit, but now the elements were far outside what I had imagined.

Sattie left no choices for the remainder of the evening. I planned for academic performance, but now I was expected to perform in another realm.

At 3 AM I shuffled to my room. Just a few hours after I had arrived back at my apartment, I presented the paper to the seminar, and indeed I received an "A."

In a single evening, she had corrupted me in mind and body and consigned me to Hell.

CHAPTER 7

A Word from Salman

Rarely hearing from Salman, I felt distanced from my father. And when Salman did reach out, it was always in the vein of putting me at an even greater distance. The letter I received in November 1961 was no exception.

Dear Yacoub,

I hope you are conserving your funds. We are sacrificing much to keep you there in a land that does not know the Holy Quran.

Much is happening here in Kuwait. The British are commencing their withdrawal. We are now responsible for much of our own legal system. I regret to tell you it is being developed along the lines of the Egyptian model. What a disaster for us. The Egyptians are relics of the Ottomans. Perhaps with your study of Sharia, you will be able to rescue us.

The British here tell us we are now independent. What does this mean? We are a tiny state among monsters. Iraq is saying we are part of the old Ottoman Empire, and therefore we now belong to them. The Emir has requested assistance from the Saudis and British and in'shallah they will help. Two British ships have appeared in the harbor.

I do not know what we would have done without your brother, Suhayb. He alone has preserved the family. He is a leader in the mosque. He has mastered the Quran and is able to recite it entirely. When the men are out together in the desert, he leads the prayers. While he does not speak as the leader in the great mosque, he is afforded the privileges of an imam. He has become close with the leaders of our fledgling military, and I am confident he would take the forward position if the Iraqis come.

I did not know he would have a mind for business, but he has taken charge of both our family's farming enterprise and also our connections with the Emir's oil company.

Suhayb now has two wives, and we are adding on to our home so that his wives and children are able to live with us. Already there are conflicts, as your mother did not approve of the tribes of his new wives. But I gave my blessing. The women do not abide in peace in our household, but then what else should we expect?

But the best is that your brother has shown himself devoted to Islam. I wish that I knew you were of the same mind.

Your father

I tried to keep my emotions intact as I read the letter, but the tone and content weighed me down. How did he know my current view of Islam? What betrayed me?

CHAPTER 8

Sharia and Me

My coursework succeeded, and Dr. Allison saw to my respect among the other professors. My language gifts were apparent to all.

So, I began my study of Sharia. I envied Suhayb's memorization of the Quran, as this base would have made my path quicker, but I soon found there was actually little that was representative of "law" in the Quran. I memorized the small number of verses specifically dealing with these issues as background for the research. As my method I set these verses up such that they were equivalent to mathematical certainty or the "gold standard" of my project. *A great idea!* From this point, my approach flowed down to the other sources of Sharia, designating those, which would be considered primary.

I then considered what constituted a primary source. My basic course in historical methodology was confusing and ridiculous in its essence. The most believable definition of a primary source was the recording by an eyewitness of event set down near the time of the observed event. But then what about sources that were designated as primary because they had been designated as such by an earlier observer, who was no longer available? And what if the primary document itself was no longer available, as was almost always the case when dealing with anything as old as Islam? The one who transmits such a document might call it primary, but was it? I found, on the strictest grounds, there were no primary sources. Frustration set in.

I was left with *fiqh*. And I knew the level of behavior to which *fiqh* had led me. Islam allowed as many as four wives at a time, but none could be the wife of another, and I had taken the wife of another, or rather the wife of another had taken me.

As I learned more about Sharia, I was not pleased with direction of my work. Dr. Allison said, "I can see your work is coming along nicely. Yacoub, please come over this afternoon." Such was her frequent request.

An afternoon at Sattie's desert hacienda was becoming routine, both from the standpoint of academic productivity, which was outstanding, and also from the standpoint of my moral surrender. I must say there were highlights, however.

The layout of the Allison home became familiar: the living room with its soft red couch, the walnut liquor cabinet in the corner, the photographs of Sattie's native American ancestors, of which she was quite proud.

"Yacoub, let's talk about where this is headed."

"Where what is headed?" I wasn't sure what she meant, the academic success or the moral decline.

"Your research, of course, what did you think I meant? You certainly don't think our little dalliance here is anything, do you? You're such a pretty boy."

Her last words stung.

"No, what I mean is your research. You must know where it's leading. Eventually you'll return to Kuwait. If they start the university there, as they have been discussing, you'll teach. Don't be naïve with me. You'd better hope they don't understand. I know where you're headed and so do you. You're still playing games in your mind and pretending you don't see the inevitable conclusion. You're well on your way to abandoning your desire to know some elusive certainty."

"I think I'm confused, or maybe afraid. I don't know which. I'm not sure what you're talking about."

"Yacoub, we're finished for the day. Just leave. Next time you come, park your car round the block."

It was the mid-year break, which coincided with the Christian holidays and the Western New Year, for the college. The university shut down for three weeks. I thought briefly about going home. *No, bad idea.* Why should I make things worse? I was glad to have some time off from my studies. Perhaps I wouldn't even have to see Sattie. Perhaps I could have some time away from the double confusion, academic and personal, she inflicted on me.

For a few days I didn't look at books or papers. I tried to regroup. But what was my objective? I had begun with the Quran and the central idea of revelation from Allah. This was the way, the only way, one could know. I thought of knowing as the central tent pole from which all else would come. I had therefore proceeded to Sharia as the rules for living, which flowed from the Quran. But the deeper I delved into the basis of Sharia, I discovered that outside the Quran, there were many versions of what was said to be true. My search for "primary sources" led me away from knowing.

What about my family in Kuwait? What about the consternation of my mother and her trouble with Salman and Suhayb and their women? Was I being selfishly intellectual in trying to remain above the fray? There were real problems for them in Kuwait, and I had created my own. Here I sat alone at Christmas in a foreign desert, self-involved, feeling sorry for myself, and failing to reach any conclusions that were representative of the intellect I thought I possessed.

Seven PM on a Wednesday night. Most of the students were gone, and those in town were with their families. I walked down to the Blue Diamond, which was empty, and sat on a barstool. The blue neon light announcing the name of the saloon flickered in the window.

"You stayin' here for Christmas, pal? Ya don't look so good."

"I'm not."

"Yer girl dump you?"

"Wish she would."

"She pregnant or somethin?"

"How'd you ever come up with that?"

"I dunno. It just came to me. I get pretty good at this stuff."

"No, definitely no. She's not that stupid."

"Sometimes it's not the gal that's stupid."

It only got worse from there, and after a few more scotches, this time without ice, I went back to my apartment.

The phone rang as I opened the door.

"Yacoub, come over this evening." It was Sattie.

"It's after eleven."

"You need to come over."

"I haven't really done anything more on the paper."

"Well we can talk about that, too, if you want."

She left me no choice.

All the lights in the house were on. Sattie's hair was fixed and she had on makeup. Unusual for her at that time of the day. She told me to sit down on the couch, and she put her arm on the couch back behind me.

"I'm sorry, but I thought I'd have more time over Christmas to work on the paper."

"Forget the paper. Yacoub, I'm pregnant. It's yours."

"But how do you know it's mine?"

"My husband and I haven't had sex for six months. I'll fix that when he comes home tomorrow night."

"I can't believe this." I thought of Anna back in London and wondered what had happened to her.

"So you can't believe this. Well isn't that something!"

"There're doctors who can fix this. I'll pay for them."

"Yacoub, I can't do that. I'm Catholic. Besides, I want the baby."

She had spent the months trying to convince me there was no way to "know" anything, no absolutes in history or in life and now, "I'm Catholic." How did this creep into the discussion?

Sattie touched my shoulder and smiled. "I'm really happy."

I looked at her red hair and white skin and then at the brown skin on the back of my hand. Not from the Arizona sun. Then, on the mantel a photo of her blond, blue-eyed husband stared down. There was going to be trouble.

For the next three months Dr. Allison was sick. Her appearance alternated between radiance and a greenish hue. Sometimes she managed to get to her classes, but mostly not. This provided a little respite for me, and I enjoyed the vacation from her. The private sessions at her home had ended.

In March Dr. Allison happily announced her pregnancy to her classes. "My husband and I are ecstatic." She said she would try to finish the semester, that she would then take the summer off, and that she would try to return sometime during the fall. But how would this affect my thesis? *Always me.*

* * *

My regular classes were in many ways repeats of the work I had done at King's College, and I was now left free to work on the framework of the thesis on the development of Sharia law. I began to lose the naïveté that had led to my confusion. I felt foolish with the thought I would be able to define the limits of Sharia in terms that were mathematically precise. My thought processes were taking a more realistic direction but one that frightened me nevertheless. But it was time to face up to the matter.

Now that I had for the moment been delivered from the clutches of Sattie, her remarks came back to me. I got around to looking up the Feast of the Saternalia. I learned this was the favorite Roman holiday, one where the slaves and masters traded places, and the masters "served" the slaves. The holiday had a beginning and an end for the Romans. For me there was no end, and I was not the master, but the slave.

The dreams returned in full force, and the white camel was again the star. The camel came out of the Arizona desert and invaded my bedroom. I tried to move and escape but still the camel came. He was a messenger with no clear message. The center of my abdomen trembled. Of what future did the beast portend? Would there be an end to these visitations? Did I even desire an end?

CHAPTER 9

Lost in Hadith

Having stipulated the statements in the Quran that formed Sharia law, I set about dealing with the subsequent sources of Sharia. For the time being, there was none of the confusion of dealing with Sattie. I should be able to handle the subject as an intellectual exercise. This state of mind opened up a broad base of investigation, and there was now a wealth of data in front of me. Though I had set about to write a PhD thesis on Sharia law, but I did not yet have a thesis to prove or defend. There were many iterations of Sharia, and it would be pointless simply to repeat one of them.

The fall of 1962 approached and my PhD committee was chosen. Of course Sattie would be one of the committee members, but the two other professors might impose some risk for me. The first chosen, Professor Glenbrook, was an expert on civil war history and knew nothing about Arabs, the Middle East, or the Quran. The other, Professor Duncan, was a recognized scholar in the area of the epistemology of historical data, the heart of my thesis. His presence on the committee made it a certainty the thesis sources would be called into question at every point. The sources of Sharia were generally thought by Western scholars to be questionable, and Duncan was known to be difficult, unyielding, and often mean-spirited.

My first meeting with the committee didn't go well. The room was too small, and I was too near my committee members. Duncan was a three-pack-a-day smoker, and the odor filled the room.

Duncan opened the first meeting by announcing that he was head of the committee. I felt my jaw drop. I expected that Sattie would be in charge.

Duncan began, "Mr. Al-Tamimi, your expression indicates your displeasure. Do you have a problem with our proceeding? If you do, this is the time to make it clear."

Sattie was quiet. From the appearance of her growing abdomen, I understood her active participation in the process was unlikely at this point.

I answered belatedly. "No, of course not, Dr. Duncan. I'm quite satisfied with the arrangements."

"Good. Let's proceed. We understand you wish to undertake your thesis on the history of Sharia law. You are probably aware I am quite interested in the authority of the documents in this specific area."

I had not been aware of the specificity. Did I look shocked?

Glenbrook piped up, "How do you intend to authenticate the sources you use?"

I responded, "Well, the Quran is the easiest."

Glenbrook replied, "Yes, of course, but the others...?"

"They're more complicated," was the best I could say.

Duncan interjected, "We see you have a long way to go. I saw your record from King's College. I expected more from you."

Sattie remained silent.

Duncan asked, "For your sources, give me your best guesses about their authenticity."

I fumbled badly. I had no satisfactory answers. "After the Quran comes the Sunnah, the examples from the life of the Prophet."

Glenbrook said, "Which prophet?" Now Glenbrook taunted me.

I responded, "Mohammed."

Duncan asked, "How will you know the Sunnah?"

"This is contained in the hadiths," I replied.

Glenbrook asked, "How many hadiths are there?

I didn't know. I guessed, "Maybe 10,000."

Duncan then asked, "And all of these are authentic?"

"I don't know, probably not."

Glenbrook asked, "How will you know?'

Duncan stopped the torture, "Well, let's stop for now. For the next meeting, we must know the answer to Dr. Glenbrook's last question, or at least we will want to know your method, and whether there is anything novel about your approach."

Sattie still had not spoken. She smiled slightly, and I saw her protruding abdomen move under her skirt.

CHAPTER 10

A Son is Born

I heard through other students that Dr. Allison had delivered. It was a boy. How should I feel? I was indeed frightened, but I had to see the child. Perhaps he would look nothing like me. Sattie's husband had never met me, but upon seeing me as one of Sattie's students, perhaps he would make the connection over a brown infant. I had to see what I was dealing with. I drove to the hospital and parked in the lot outside the three-story building. I hesitated in the car for several minutes and then took the elevator up to the third floor and waited around the nursery to make sure her husband was not about. I then went down the rows of babies visible through the large window.

Perhaps Allison was Sattie's professional name, which meant I might not identify the baby by the husband's name. But there he was. There could be no doubt. There was only one dark skinned infant, last name Gundersen. I went straight for baby Gundersen and looked into his dark eyes. My feet were transported above the floor as my attack hit, and I collapsed in front of the nursery glass. I was not unconscious, though it appeared so, and I tried to gather myself to my feet before anyone saw me. I didn't succeed. Several nurses rushed to my aid, checking my heart rate, ready to employ their resuscitation skills, and then helping me up when recovery was evident. One of them had seen me staring at the baby. "Mr. Gundersen, you certainly have a beautiful son, so handsome," she said.

"I'm not Mr. Gundersen."

"Oh, I thought...." Her voice trailed off and she looked at the baby and then back at me directly. I was certain she knew. The nurse had stopped smiling.

"Thanks for helping me. I just tripped." Neither nurse responded.

Then I saw Gundersen getting off the elevator. I recognized him from the photograph over Sattie's mantel, and I retreated around the corner and sought refuge in the stairwell. I had to speak to Sattie, and ask what they were going to do. I must be in trouble. I cowered in the stairwell considering all alternate plans. For three hours I camped in the stairwell, periodically peering out at the door of Sattie's room. Finally Gundersen left and got on the elevator. I went to the window of the third floor and watched Gundersen get into his car and depart for the evening.

I left the stairwell and headed for Sattie's room. The nurse who had called me 'Mr. Gundersen' saw me and looked me straight in the eye.

Sattie awoke when I entered.

"Yacoub, what the hell are you doing here? Have you lost your mind? My husband just left."

"I had to see."

"Well, you've seen, now get out of here."

"But I've got to know, does he know?"

"No, he does not know, but he has never seen you, and it would be best if he never saw you."

"How could he not know? The baby is as brown as me."

"I have Indian blood on my side of the family. A lot of Arizonans have that. Besides, he wants the baby to be his. Our secret is safe for the moment. Now get out of here."

I left, took one last look at our son in the nursery, and went home to bed. There was no sleep. I didn't understand the nuances

Dr. Duncan was asking me to pursue, but I knew that in my time out of Kuwait I had broken the laws of the Prophet. I had planned the murder of the baby I fathered with Anna. I had committed adultery. I had lied, and these lies were due to be compounded. And here I was writing a PhD thesis on Sharia law.

CHAPTER 11

How Did This Happen?

H ow did I get into this thesis? All I wanted to do was study Sharia, which must be the basis of God-approved law. Knowing the hadiths constituted much of the basis for Sharia, I settled on them for my PhD thesis. Surely this was enough. And now my preceptors asked for a method to accomplish the project.

Finally I had an idea. But where it would lead?

At the next meeting of my committee, Sattie was absent. She would likely be indisposed for several months. Only Duncan and Glenbrook were present.

The smokey Duncan began, "Well, Mr. Al-Tamimi, what have you decided about your approach to the hadiths? This is the sole purpose of our meeting, so we should get to it. If you are not ready, as was the case for our last meeting, we can reconvene again later."

"No, sir, I'm prepared. The 'Authentic Six' is considered the authoritative rendition of Sunni Islam in regard to the sayings of the Prophet. I've decided on a method that differs from the methods used by the 'Authentic Six.' I will assume they are correct in the application of the approach they used. But I will focus only on the *Sahih Al-Bukhari*, the first of the six."

I knew that Duncan and Glenbrook had familiarized themselves with the structure of the hadiths, so they understood the general idea so far.

Glenbrook asked, "I assume you accept Al-Bukhari's method as wholly accurate. After all, he did trace the individual hadiths through specific lines of transmission."

"Of course." I responded positively for the sake of simplicity, but there would be complicating issues.

"Alright, what's the rest of your approach?"

"I will examine the hadiths of Al-Bukhari from a linguistic standpoint, using the grammar and vocabulary of the Quran as the standard. Those hadiths with Quranic grammar construction and Quranic vocabulary would be given the highest degree of authenticity."

"Well, I believe that is a novel approach," said Glenbrook.

Duncan interjected, "Yes, but none of us on this committee have the sufficient knowledge of Arabic to handle that portion of the project. And even in our university there are no scholars in the Arabic language."

Glenbrook said, "I think I might have a solution. We can convene again in about two weeks." I had not considered this as a problem. What was Glenbrook's solution?

The two weeks passed and finally I was called to meet. I entered the office and in addition to Duncan and Glenbrook there was a gentleman sitting quietly in typical Saudi dress but with a beard much longer than normal and a dishdasha up above his ankles. His appearance suggested severely conservative Islam.

"Yacoub, please meet Professor Abdulatif Al-Ghabani from the University of Colorado. Dr. Ghabani is a professor of Arabic there." Al-Ghabani did not make eye contact.

What were the dangers Al-Ghabani might impose? I struggled to recall the name Al-Ghabani. Then, it came to me. Al-Ghabani was a scholar and fundamentalist Islamist of the Hanbali School of Sharia, its most conservative branch. Definitely a blow. Now

I was facing both academic and ecclesiastical problems. How could I navigate this religious sea? That Al-Ghabani had accepted the assignment was no coincidence. I was certain he understood the implications in advance.

Al-Ghabani was quiet and smiling pleasantly during the meeting. Nothing came up that seemed threatening, and they agreed on my approach and dispersed.

I took comfort at the benign character of the meeting and began to make my way back to the apartment.

But outside the history building under the large pine, Al-Ghabani was waiting for me. His pleasant demeanor had evaporated.

"Well, young man, what do you think you're doing?"

"I intend to use the linguistic method I outlined to study the hadiths."

"Don't be naïve with me. You know what you're doing. Your approach is filled with danger. And I must tell you the danger is all your own. The hadiths exist on their own merits. If you challenge them, you bring yourself to apostasy."

"I don't understand."

"If you don't understand, you are in even more danger than I thought."

"I just need a method to do my thesis."

"Your thesis will take you to hell. Look, I know your family in Kuwait. Do you want to dishonor them?"

"No, of course not."

"You've already set your course. Now you must navigate it. There are rocks on both sides. If you question the legitimacy of Al-Bukhari's hadiths, there will be no end to what you've begun. Look, my young friend, I know this is just an academic exercise. No one beyond this committee will ever read your PhD thesis. You'd better hope they don't."

"Yes sir, I'll be careful. Thank you very much for all your concern. I know you have my best interests in mind." Was I condescending?

"I have no interest in you. My only interest is the word of Allah. If you attempt to disparage it, I'll finish your career before it begins. I know they're going to start a university in Kuwait. You must plan to return there to teach. If they need to hear of your academic mischief, I will make sure they do hear. Carry out your little childish exercise and make as little noise as possible." He didn't wait for a response. He got back into his rental Chevrolet and departed.

I was stunned by the severity of Al-Ghabani's remarks, but I had little choice but to proceed. I was lost in the land of epistemology. How foolish had I been? My first step was simply a careful study of the Quran from a linguistic standpoint. Of course I had read the Quran many times but not from this critical position. I armed myself with a dictionary of ancient Arabic and a copy of *Wright's Arabic Grammar.*

I had never spent such intensive time with the Quran, and I came to admire the grace and grandeur of the text. As a literary work alone it was of unsurpassed beauty of language. I had always accepted the work at its face value as the work of Allah, and now I was comfortable with the quality of language. I put aside the issue of inspiration or Allah-dictation of the work, but my altruistic idea of "knowing" remained intact for the moment.

I immersed myself in the grammar and compiled a vocabulary list of words that were unique to the Quran or at least rarely used in other sources. I then embarked on investigation of the *Sahih Al-Bukhari.* The rare texts required I spend hours among the dusty volumes of the university library. Even though the books were rarely used, they were considered too valuable to be removed from the library.

My task was now to review over 4000 hadiths. I set about this work that would require nearly the next two years. I arrived at a numerical score sheet to use as the scale for his project. Rare words, which were mainly used the Quran, were the primary measure. Those hadiths that contained such vocabulary were awarded the highest position. The grammar, including word endings and diacritical marks employed in the Quran, was the secondary measure. The diacritical marks were given less weight, as they did not exist in the earliest transcripts of the Quran.

The intensity and rigor of the work served to blur my concern about the philosophic certainty of what I was doing. Only occasionally did my mind drift back to what I had considered as certainty when I first embarked on this road. But the mental confusion, the dichotomy of belief and unbelief, hung as a smoldering fire.

My newly acquired friend and fellow grad student, Philip, provided some relief. He was studying the history of the southwestern Indian tribes and their religious practices, so there was some affiliation in this respect. Philip was also a practicing Christian, the first I had ever encountered.

"Yacoub, why don't you join me for church on Sunday?"

"I'd feel odd going. Wouldn't it be a bit dishonest?"

Philip responded, "Only if church attendance is dishonest for all."

Sunday morning came, and I was uncertain of what I should wear. I settled on a new blue sport coat and red tie. Philip picked me up wearing a short sleeve shirt and slacks. We pulled up in the parking lot of the Church of the Holy Ghost and the Empty Sepulcher.

What did the name of the church signify? What did a ghost have to do with Christianity? Christians didn't believe in ghosts, do they? And why the idea of a sepulcher? A sepulcher is a place for the dead. What is the value of an empty grave, a grave that has no contents?

We entered the narthex of the church, which was red brick with a tall steeple. Philip was warmly greeted with embraces. The steeple reminded me of a minaret.

The service began, and the preacher was loud with much repetition, which was greeted with voiced agreement and raised arms from the congregation. The whole procedure was disorderly, nothing like the regular proceedings of Muslim worship. The congregation began to sing, and their voices were joyful and the words repetitive. The exultation of the moment exceeded everything I had ever observed in the mosque. While the events in the mosque emphasized our impassable distance from God, it was clear the congregants felt they had breached that gap.

Finally, after plates were passed to collect money, the preacher began to speak. He first read a passage from the third chapter of the book of John, which made absolutely no sense to me. How could a man be born again? And what did water and a ghost have to do with the whole matter? After the preacher had spoken loudly for thirty minutes, some in the congregation began to cry, and the pastor asked a number to come forward for a process that he called by several names: confession, profession, and finally conversion. At intervals during the activity, the preacher invoked the intervention of the "Holy Ghost." I did not see the ghost.

What were they being converted from and converted to? Apparently through some process they were actually becoming Christians when they had not been so previously. How could this be? I was born a Muslim. No change was required.

After the service concluded, the crowd dispersed out to the church lawn where they engaged in more smiling conversations and embraces. I was pleasantly included in this along with Philip. They spoke to me as if I was one of them. At length a kind looking, small gray-haired women approached and asked Philip and me to lunch.

"Young man, are you from around Tucson?" Because of my brown skin she likely thought I was an American Indian.

"No ma'am, I'm from Kuwait."

"Oh wonderful, it's so good to meet a Christian from another part of the world."

"Actually, I'm Muslim."

"You must tell me about that. What God do you believe in?"

"It's the same as yours."

"Oh no, young man. That's not possible. Come along to my house. Follow my car."

We arrived at a small, well-kept house with old furniture. The cloth covering the couch was worn through in places. The meal had been prepared earlier and we set down at the dining room table covered with a linen tablecloth that was clean but with old gravy stains. Despite the potential theological argument that could have brewed, conflict was avoided. The atmosphere enveloped me with a feeling of harmony. A large pork roast was brought out along with well-cooked potatoes, carrots and rolls. Before its aroma entrapped me, Philip warned me about the source of the meat. I was able to get through the meal without further awkwardness.

Philip and I did not speak as we drove back to the university. I really didn't know what to say, but I was oddly content and relaxed.

And one more point: the more I attended the church, the less frequently the camel came to me. What did the camel fear? Or was he disgusted with my fraud?

CHAPTER 12

Al-Ghabani's Visitation

Sunday was a day when there was little to do at the university, and many stores were closed. There was no mosque in Tucson yet, and if there had been, I would have had to go on Fridays anyway. I thus fell into the routine of going to church with Philip. The people there were friendly and didn't force their religion upon me. Perhaps Philip was responsible for this. I sometimes got a meal after church at someone's home.

Still, even after going for a number of Sundays, their practices completely baffled me. Many of the songs were repetitive, and in that way not unlike the sameness of worship in the mosque, but the attendees were jubilant in performing them. What elevated their mood? Sometimes there were tears in response to the music. In the mosque, there was little expression of emotion. Often there was a raising of hands in the church. I understood how physicality might be a part of worship. I knew that from the actions of Muslim prayer, but here it seemed spontaneous. *From the heart and not the rules?* Then, there were those individuals who would speak in a language that did not appear to have any rational meaning. This was tolerated and even encouraged by the pastor. At the end of the service, the pastor usually invited people to come forward for prayer. This practice did not seem to arise from any plan. This event for the individual was referred to as "conversion," which implied a change, but of a type unknown to me.

But the most striking events were those that occurred irregularly; not every service, usually during a visit by another preacher. The visiting preacher would ask for any in the congregation who were sick to come forward for, as he put it, "the healing of the Holy Ghost." So again there was this thing about a "ghost." After the pastor prayed while touching the person, the individual often fell, only to rise stating that he or she was "healed." The congregation thrived on the experience, and even as a non-involved observer, I felt uplifted.

I attended whenever I could break away from the thesis work.

* * *

The time came round for another meeting of my PhD committee. It was Friday. All four of the faculty preceptors were present this time. Dr. Allison had returned from her pregnancy leave. She showed pictures of the little boy to the other faculty but not to me.

Al-Ghabani had flown in for the meeting from Denver, and the members of the committee inquired about the progress of the work, which was favorable. I had sent Al-Ghabani some of the work on the linguistics. Al-Ghabani gave his approval of the quality of the work with his compliments on its accuracy, but he didn't make eye contact with me. I left the meeting contented. The trouble with Al-Ghabani was over. He seemed to have surrendered to the need for the academic exercise.

That weekend I went back to the Church of the Holy Ghost and Empty Sepulcher and came out relaxed and contented, as usual. Then, I saw him. Al-Ghabani was parked at the curb. He motioned for me to get into the car, and we drove off. Al-Ghabani stopped the car at a nearby park, and we got out and sat at a picnic table across from one another. I had not spoken.

"Well, Yacoub, I suspected something like this was going on." He was unsmiling and now making full eye contact. "Is there anything you can say in your defense? I knew from your work in the hadiths that you were challenging the authority of Islam. I was afraid there might be something more to it than scholarship."

"So you followed me?"

"Yes, I followed you. It was my responsibility as a defender of the truth."

"What happens now?"

"It depends on how far this has gone. You know the penalty for leaving Islam. And I can promise you, I will see it is enforced—not now, of course, but when you return to Kuwait."

"I have not left Islam."

"Then you must stop going to this church, or whatever it is."

"Alright."

"And I know your family in Kuwait. The 'Aniza are an honored tribe. They must be informed of your ecclesiastical philandering. I will go to Kuwait and speak with your father."

"No, you can't do that!"

"Yacoub, I don't know which is worse, your PhD topic or your attending this church. Frankly, I suspect it's the former. I think it represents a serious defect in your mind that will be difficult to repair. Your father and brother may be able to intervene on your behalf."

"My father won't understand about the thesis."

"Perhaps your brother will. I hear that he has reached the status of imam. So, I'm flying to Kuwait next week. I'll expect to see you there with your family. You must face this."

I would have to miss classes for a week. I was still afraid of Suhayb, and he would relish the opportunity to delve into this. I swam in treacherous waters, and I thought I could dog paddle through them. I was wrong.

I needed a plan to correct the problem. It would be complicated but I could do it. My skill in language had always rescued me in the past. I would go back to Kuwait as a conservative proponent of Sharia. To do so, I would have to skirt around Al-Ghabani. And I would also need to outsmart Suhayb, which wouldn't be hard. But there were indeed those in Kuwait who would kill over what they deemed apostasy.

I prepared to leave quickly in order to arrive at my home before Al-Ghabani. The morning of my departure, I again experienced the paralysis during early morning awakening. My inability to move was more prolonged than usual. And there was a visitation of the white camel, and on this occasion the white camel was smiling, if a camel can smile. His "smile," or perhaps a snarl, revealed a black mole on his inner, briefly exposed, lower lip.

That morning before the departure I looked over my research folder, in desperation more than for any other reason. I then made a discovery before I left for the airport; a discovery that was to make my trip much more agreeable.

I got off the plane and proceeded quickly through immigration, where there was a special desk for the easy entry of Kuwaiti citizens. I took a cab to the International Hotel along Gulf Road where I knew Al-Ghabani would be staying, and I called Al-Ghabani's room from the lobby phone. My heart beat rapidly.

"Professor, may I come up to speak with you?"

"I suppose so, but we have nothing to talk about. You've done the damage, and now the information must be passed to your family. May Allah have mercy upon you, because I will not."

I went up the elevator, knocked on the door and Al-Ghabani, dressed in a white terry cloth bathrobe, opened the door. "Professor, thank you for seeing me. I am very grateful for this opportunity." Did Al-Ghabani perceive my intended sarcastic tone?

"What do you want?"

"I want just a moment of your time to discuss my work on the thesis."

"You can't be serious! It's a bit late to pursue this. As I've said, the damage is done by the fact you have initiated this process, you apostate."

"Allow me just a moment. I want to discuss how your famous paper, 'The Well-Spring of Life in the Language of the Quran,' has greatly illuminated my thinking."

"This flattery now is of no value to your cause. I've already received acclaim among the experts in the area, of which you are not one. The paper was the main thing responsible for my promotion to full professor."

"Professor, I'm fully aware of the cause of your fame and success in academia."

"Yacoub, your words are complimentary but your tone is not. Are you asking for an even more terrible outcome than the one that is already headed your way? I have friends in Kuwait who can put an end to your doings."

"Hear me out, please, professor. I think you'll agree I've made an important discovery. I switched from Arabic to English. I believe you are familiar with the work of the great Syrian linguist, Saher Al-Muthari, and in particular his work, 'The Reach of Lofty Language,' depending of course how one translates 'lofty.' And I know you have made your own English translation of the work, especially since a published English translation does not exist. Strangely, I did not see Al-Muthari among the works of those you cited in your paper."

Al-Ghabani moved back from the edge of his chair and pulled a pillow onto his lap. Now he was silent.

I purposely changed my tone of voice to controlled and derisive. "Professor, there is a very interesting and quite long passage in Al-Muthari's paper, and once again, quite strangely, the passage, after direct translation into English, is identical with a very long passage in your famous paper."

Al-Ghabani did not speak.

"Of course, there was no danger in anyone sorting this out at the University of Colorado or in American peer review. Who among them would read Al-Muthari's paper on linguistics that has been published only in Arabic? Your indiscretion was low risk. Until I came along."

Still there was no word from Al-Ghabani.

"So, professor, this is what we shall do. I will agree to refrain from revealing your plagiarism as long as you refrain from revealing what you deem as my apostasy. We will go and have an amicable visit with my family. I trust you will be complimentary about my high level of scholarship. After all, that's why you came to Kuwait, to inform my family of my outstanding performance, isn't it? For you not to visit them, after you've told them you were coming, would be an affront. So will you visit, yes?"

"I believe I can do that."

"And lastly you will support my thesis and performance in my studies in the most favorable manner."

"Are we finished here?"

"Yes, thank you for your time. Tomorrow evening we will welcome you at the home of my family as an honored guest."

I spent the next day at home with my family. The decline in my mother and father startled me. Salman was no longer getting around easily, and Fatima, while she was physically well, was clearly depressed and no longer herself. The time during the day with my parents went slowly and sadly. They had converted my old room to a storage closet.

Suhayb came in at noon from his adjoining villa. He was robust and controlling of the situation, as if Salman had already abdicated his position as head of the family. Suhayb's physical demeanor had already been imposing and now was even more so with his increased confidence over his success in running the family businesses. His newfound religious recognition accentuated all aspects. He greeted me enthusiastically.

"Well Yacoub, I'm happy to see you. We did not expect you. Will you be staying long?"

"No, I'm just in Kuwait for a few days. I must return to my classes. One of my professors was eager to come and inform you of my progress."

"Is this the Saudi from University of Colorado, Al-Ghabani? He's highly thought of among the imams in Kuwait. I'll be honored to meet him."

"He's coming tonight."

Al-Ghabani arrived at 8 PM and was ushered by the farash into the greeting room. The men were there to greet him. The women were listening in the adjoining room behind the divider curtain.

Suhayb began, "Professor, we're honored by your visit. Thank you for coming." He had taken the part of Salman in being the chief greeter.

I joined in, erasing my sarcastic tone of the previous day. "Yes, professor, I'm grateful for your visit." How would Al-Ghabani handle the situation?

"I wanted to stop by on my way to Jeddah to inform you of your son's remarkable progress. Not only is he exceeding all praise in his academic work, but his work will be a landmark in the study of Sharia and a great contribution to Islam." He lied aloud as easily as he had committed plagiarism.

That was the way evening went, and the initial excitement lapsed into boredom. Al-Ghabani met my requirements and departed with a sullen glance toward me.

Suahyb was impressed that the Saudi professor had thought my performance was of sufficient importance to come to Kuwait just to let them know. Suhayb, with little regard for subtlety, had not detected anything unusual in Al-Ghabani's demeanor.

As I departed Kuwait the next morning, I encountered Al-Ghabani in the first-class lounge at the airport on his way back to Jeddah. We did not speak or make eye contact.

CHAPTER 13

First Relief and Then . . .

I arrived back in Tucson more relaxed than I could recall. I had escaped the Al-Ghabani disaster with ease and grace. I took a cab back from the airport to my apartment and immediately fell asleep, and I awoke the next morning feeling refreshed but still sluggish from the many time zone changes. I needed fresh groceries so I went out in the early morning sun and got into my car.

I remembered nothing more until I felt the handcuffs being placed on my wrists. The officer guided me into the back of the police car. I looked over at my white Chevrolet bent round a telephone pole, and then I saw the crumpled bicycle and a little boy being covered with a sheet. He was then placed in the ambulance. The vehicle did not use its flashing lights and pulled away slowly. The police were not smiling.

"A little early in the day for gettin' drunk, eh fella?"

"I haven't had any alcohol."

"Yeah, we'll see about that."

Not much later, I sat in a small cell and after several hours, a young attorney came in stating that he had been "assigned" to my case.

"Why am I here?"

"You mean you don't know?"

"I know I had a wreck with my car. What happened to the little boy on the bicycle?"

"You here in the first place because you hit him with your car. Now you're here because he's dead."

I couldn't speak. If I had not been sitting down, I would have fallen in one of my attacks.

"You're being charged with manslaughter. I'm here to defend you."

"I don't remember anything."

"You've got to tell me more than that or I can't help you."

"I must have gone to sleep. It's happened to me before but never while I was driving."

"You have to tell me everything."

"Look, I've told you all I know." My mind raced for a plan. Surely this wasn't happening, and I would find a way out.

"You'll be taken to the court in the morning."

All I could think about was how my father could help. "Please contact my father in Kuwait. Here's a number to call." How quickly I had passed over the issue of the dead boy. All my previous high-minded thoughts of getting at the roots of Islamic law were subverted to my desire to escape from this mess. It was an exodus from the law. Any thoughts of the legalities or morality of the matter, and the taking of a young life, evaporated in my need for self-preservation.

"I need to know more of this business about your going to sleep."

"It happens to me sometimes. Please, just get my father."

The day passed in the cell. Was I losing my mind? How could this happen right after my victory?

Then, finally, the next morning an attorney with graying hair and neatly trimmed mustache appeared. He was much older than the young man of the day before. His blue suit was well tailored and probably expensive.

"My name is Allen Benedict. I'm your lawyer now. I don't want you to say anything."

"But my father..."

"Your father is going to see this is taken care of. Just don't talk to anyone about this."

Two hours later I was released. I learned that what was called "bail" had been paid and that I must return for a trial. The older lawyer met me at the door of the county jail.

"You need to go back to your school now and do your work. They've set a trial date, but there won't be a trial. Your father is a very rich man."

"What about the boy I hit?"

"I told you not to talk about this anymore. Don't you understand? The boy's family was very poor. Now, they're not poor anymore."

I picked up a newspaper and looked for the story. On one of the inside pages, there was a small grade school photo of the little boy. The story was that he had been killed crossing against the traffic light. I was not mentioned. I walked back to the site of the accident. There was no traffic light.

In the West, such payoffs were considered bribes. In the Middle East, however, this was blood money, a concept familiar to the Al-Tamimi family and the 'Aniza tribe. Really, it was simple, expensive but simple, and predating Mohammed.

And so in this search for Sharia and the real law, I benefitted by tradition in a way I had not imagined.

* * *

My thoughts quickly turned back to Al-Ghabani. I was certain Al-Ghabani was tamed by the threat of having his plagarism reported to the University of Colorado. But perhaps I underestimated the seriousness of his threat. I knew I had angered the Saudi and increased the possible penalty. And it occurred to me that to damage Al-Ghabani's reputation also had the potential of damaging the credibility of my thesis. What if the same occurred to Al-Ghabani?

In the first week after returning from Kuwait and the conclusion of the auto accident incident, I returned to the church. I had absolutely no understanding of the goings-on there, but it was a perceived refuge. My favorite among the older women asked me for lunch with a group. As I drove to her house, I wondered if I was being followed, but I dismissed the concern. The main course was a nice pork roast, which I consumed out of politeness and a vigorous appetite. *So much for that part of the law, too.*

As I drove back to the college, I was certain I was being followed. Upon exiting my new car (the first vehicle being totaled in the accident), I was approached by a dark-skinned man with a curly beard. The man was dressed in t-shirt and jeans, which somehow did not look appropriate.

"So you're Yacoub Al-Tamimi." It was a statement, not a question.

"Yes."

"Do you renounce Islam?"

"No."

"By your attendance at this church you renounce Islam. I am here to tell you the penalty for this is death. Professor Al-Ghabani brings his greetings." The man pivoted, went back to his car and drove off.

I realized that, as much importance as I had attached to the Al-Ghabani episode, I had totally misread the potential course of events. I went back to the apartment, locked the door, closed the blinds and turned down the lights. The next morning I went to a local sporting goods shop and purchased a .45 caliber revolver, an instrument I was totally unprepared to use. It was black and too heavy. I had no idea how to operate the weapon, but at least I would have it.

The dead little boy was forgotten.

That night I went to sleep with difficulty, but upon awakening, I was briefly paralyzed, and again the white camel visited. He was always there when my sins needed cover. I needed a permanent resolution regardless of the cost. Even with the gun, I couldn't bring myself to physical violence. So I went to my books and research papers, and, seemingly at the guidance of the camel, I found what I was looking for.

The next meeting of the research committee was two weeks later. I guarded my movements with care and changed travel routes often. Al-Ghabani was not present for the meeting. The meeting itself was routine and had no real purpose, as was the case for most thesis meetings. It was merely a necessity to record a convening in order to comply with university regulations for the PhD degree. This was the time to release the necessary information.

I interrupted Duncan and began, "I have some difficult news."

I read from Al-Ghabani's famous paper, "The Well-Spring of Life in Language of the Quran." I turned rapidly to the Al-Muthari paper in Arabic and read the identical passage in English.

The committee, all three, were silent, none wanting immediately to confirm the academically fatal charge of plagiarism.

I then proceeded to my recent discovery and again read another portion of Al-Ghabani's long paper. Following this passage I read from a little-known author, also never translated from the Arabic and therefore undiscoverable by those illiterate in Arabic. Al-Ghabani had been clever enough to see that his own paper had never been translated into Arabic, so that there would be none to make the crossover connection until now. I quoted a long passage from the little-known Jordanian writer, Hassan Al-Jaweri. The correspondence was complete between the two works.

Glenbrook broke the dam. "I'm astounded! Are these authors cited in the Professor's paper?"

"No, they're not."

One occurrence of plagiarism in an academician's work was bad enough, but now they knew of two. And if there were two, they all knew there were more. The crime was addictive. It would be just a matter of finding them.

Duncan interjected, "I suppose it's our responsibility to report this to his university."

Finally, Dr. Allison spoke up, "Of course we have to do that. And we have to give Yacoub the credit for finding and reporting this to us. It's clear he did this at his own academic risk and in an honorable fashion. He did this knowing it will delay the progress of his own work." Sattie and I made brief eye contact. Did she know of the underlying events?

The matter moved quickly for Al-Ghabani. The textual evidence was clear and the University of Colorado Ethics Committee had ample reason to dismiss the disgraced Al-Ghabani for cause. The fact that he had managed, at one time or another, to insult most of his colleagues rendered the process satisfying. A further investigation of his work uncovered several similar departures. Not only was Al-Ghabani stripped of his academic title but of also of his reputation in Saudia Arabia as one who had achieved success in American academics. He had dishonored the Saudi name.

It took several weeks for all this to transpire. First there had been the apostasy accusation. Was it merely an accusation? Perhaps I was indeed an apostate. Then, there was the death of the little boy. And finally there was the death threat from Al-Ghabani. And now the dark, bearded man who had been dogging me had disappeared. The Al-Ghabani threat had been quashed by the great professor's own academic adultery.

CHAPTER 14

Can I See the Ghost?

I returned to the church the next weekend. Why did I go back? Perhaps it was because of the satisfying fellowship. Perhaps the religious aspects attracted me. Or more likely it was simply because I now had the freedom to do so with Al-Ghabani out of the picture, and I flouted my freedom.

The preacher chose his text from the prophecy of Joel. He first read the passage: "I will pour out my Spirit on all flesh; your sons and daughters shall prophesy, your old men shall dream dreams, and your young men shall see visions. Even on the male and female servants in those days I will pour out my Spirit. And I will show wonders in the heavens and on the earth, blood and fire and columns of smoke. The sun will be turned to darkness and the moon to blood, before the great and awesome day of the Lord comes. And it shall come to pass that everyone who calls on the name of the Lord will be saved." The man sitting next to me saw I didn't have a Bible. He placed his text between himself and me so I had little choice but to read.

The text did not raise in me any deep understanding, as the others around seemed to draw. First, here was a mention of the "Spirit," by which I understood a reference to the "Ghost." *Jinn* were sometimes mentioned in Islam, and always in the context of evil spirits. The idea predated Mohammed, and jinn were mentioned more frequently by less educated Arabs. Why would it be desirable for this spirit to be poured out on men? Then, there was the mention of visions. I had experienced visions, not with regularity, but often. While the visions sometimes had a pleasurable or rewarding quality, surely these were not the essence of being a "Christian." The mention of the visitation of the spirit on servants as a secondary event suggested there were slaves at the time. Did Christians approve the keeping of slaves? I had never seen or heard of the sun turned to blood. Had this been observed elsewhere? Finally, there was the reference to "Lord." By now I had learned that Western Christians often referred to Allah as Lord. I was troubled. Is the "Spirit" held in the same esteem as "Lord"? The first thing I repeated from memory as a small child was the Shahada: "There is no god but God, and Mohammed is the messenger of God," emphasizing the oneness and unique nature of God. The passage the preacher had just read was a repudiation of the Shahada. Perhaps Al-Ghabani was right all along.

The service was even longer than usual, and the components of the service gradually became more dramatic. The preacher began to make imprecations for the spirit or "Ghost" to act among the congregation. Periodically this activity took the form of a member collapsing into the arms of other members with gesticulations of emotional satisfaction. I resented the ongoing activity as it became more disorganized. It was disrespectful to Allah. But the joy was unmistakable, and it grasped me.

Then, a folding chair collapsed behind me suddenly as one of the falling members brushed against it. This surprising loud sound, out of my line of vision, affected me the same way I had experienced previously. My legs collapsed and I went down in a heap. There was no one to catch me, and I hit the floor loudly enough to attract the attention of the entire church. A number in the congregation began thanking God for "saving" me, an event many in the congregation had prayed for many weeks. My falling "in the Spirit" was a clear sign to them this had occurred. What did the loss of body tone and falling signify? I had experienced exactly the same thing on other occasions with loud, surprising sounds. The event had nothing to do with "the Spirit," of this I was certain. Still, the bliss of the moment lingered with me, and I was puzzled. What had occurred?

One by one a number in the congregation approached me after the service. "We're so thankful you received the Holy Spirit." And "now you are one of us."

I knew I was not one of them, and I couldn't lie to them or myself. The fact is that I wanted to be one of them. I had seen their joy, and I desired it. But it was not so.

I politely declined a Sunday dinner invitation, got in my car and drove away. I would not return to the Church of the Holy Ghost and Empty Sepulcher.

CHAPTER 15

Forward?

D r. Allison, following Al-Ghabani's forced departure, essentially took charge of the thesis committee. She re-
organized the structure of the committee and invited
another outside Arabic linguistics expert, Dr. Alisha Edwards,
from the University of Utah. Dr. Edwards had grown up in Jor-
dan with missionary parents from the Dutch Reformed Church.
Fluent in Arabic from childhood, she was now at the top of her
field in an area with few Westerners and fewer women. She was
no threat to me as I walked the tightrope between academic
pursuit and faithfulness to Islam. For the next few years, until
I returned to Kuwait, I was my only real critic as I stumbled
between the dogmatic interpretations of Sharia and what my
research taught me.

The short version of what happened over the next two years
with the thesis is that it was successful and led to my being
awarded a PhD in Islamic history with an emphasis in Sharia law.

My discovery was that fully 40 percent of the hadiths I studied showed linguistic characteristics of a date much later than
had been originally thought. I refrained from drawing conclusions from this result such that the roots of Islam would be perturbed, but rather left this open for the further interpretation.
But the significance of the finding was obvious. And there was

no serious question about my acceptance onto the faculty of Kuwait University. The fact that I received a PhD from an American university was sufficient. And just as Al-Ghabani had predicted, probably no one at Kuwait University would read the thesis.

After completion of the thesis, I had intended to return to Kuwait right away, but the opening of the university was delayed two years until 1966, and I was without a plan for the intervening time. The dilemma was solved in an unusual and slightly embarrassing way. A large donation was made to the University of Arizona in the name of the Al-Tamimi family of which I was to be the principal beneficiary. I was therefore given a teaching position of Assistant Professor, a level my academic credentials did not justify. I knew this and so did my new colleagues. Duncan smirked at me in faculty meetings.

I had been surprised at how easily the judicial system and the family of the boy I had killed had been bought off. How was the Al-Tamimi family doing so well? Now with the major donation to the University of Arizona, their wealth eclipsed my expectations.

A letter from my father elaborated.

Dear Yacoub,

In your absence, Allah has blessed us beyond our hopes. The Emir Abdullah III has been masterful in his developing the riches of the country. While the independence from the British in 1961 did not make much difference initially, those of us who were privileged quickly took advantage of the new economic conditions. Not the least of these was Suhayb who now leads us in the business. The people all begin to talk in the souq when they see him coming with his red hair and charismatic demeanor. He has proven himself a leader both in business and as an imam. There is talk he will soon be in the Emir's cabinet.

The Iraqis initially indicated they might annex Kuwait as their Basra province, but this was skillfully turned aside, at least for the time. Suhayb has taken a strong and outspoken position in the local press against the possible Iraqi incursion. He is often seen at the residence of the Emir.

If you return to us, perhaps there will be some role for you in Kuwait.

With the blessings of Allah,

Salman.

I had been deposed.

My duties for the next two years were minimal teaching assignments, one course in basic conversational Arabic, which drew only a handful of students, and another in Islamic history. There was no more Al-Ghabani, no more legal problems over the terrible accident, and no more worries over the child I spawned with Sattie. Sometimes I drove down to the park to watch my son from a distance but that was all. Sattie would not let me get nearer.

There was no point in my returning to Kuwait until the new university there opened, and my two classes required little work. The conversational Arabic course was really a waste of time for all. The students couldn't converse, and I couldn't make them do so. The Modern Middle East history course also required little preparation, and almost anything in the area was new information to his students. It was like I was teaching them about the history of Mars. There were several outspoken Christians in the class, and their main interest was the birth of the Jewish state in 1948. They were fixated on the idea this event was the culmination of Old Testament prophesy, an issue in which I had only passing interest and even less confidence. The students were dismayed to learn that the back-channel setting for the event had been developed by two lower level, inexperienced diplomats, Mark Sykes, the Brit, and Georges Picot of France, that the British had essentially promised the land of Palestine to the Jews in the Balfour declaration of 1917, and that the whole episode was really a political boondoggle on the part of the Great Powers in what they called the Great Game. Several of the students were actually offended by the real history.

I was left free of mind for the two-year period. This was my chance to explore relaxed thoughts about the roots of Islam and what all this really meant. While I could relegate much of my thinking to academics, what troubled me still was my initial idea that, if I got to the underlying principles of Islam, as mainly conveyed in the Quran, then I would be able to know the truth for certain in the philosophical sense. But I always failed. I stumbled over my stumbling. Once the camel visited and laughed at me.

A mosque opened in Tucson. There were few attendees, but I was often one of them. Perhaps by observing the ritual practices of Islam, I might find the truths contained therein. This did not happen, and I asked for an appointment with the new imam. He was a kindly, older man with white beard who received me warmly.

"The blessings of Allah to you!"

"Thanks very much for receiving me, Talal. I'm thankful Allah has brought you to us. I have some questions. They're rather personal, and I ask for your strict confidence." How much should I expose my uncertainty and possible apostasy? I wanted no more of the likes of Al-Ghabani or his henchmen.

We went into the imam's study and sat across from one another in green, heavily cushioned chairs. "I assure you our time together is completely secure and private."

"I would like to ask you how you yourself became convicted of the truth of Islam." I feared going further. Perhaps even this question went too far.

"That's a very easy question. I was born an observer of Islam, a Muslim. There has never been a time when there was anything else. There will never be anything else. Allah has given his final word."

This was not a satisfactory answer to a philosophical question, but I didn't know how to press the issue. I had asked the wrong question by couching it in a personal way.

I tried again, "For any Muslim what is the cause or root of being convicted of Islam?"

Talal looked puzzled and disappointed. I had exposed my apostasy. I was sinking with the weight of philosophy while Talal simply dealt with external facts.

"You became a Muslim because you are a Muslim. There is nothing more and nothing less to it." Talal persisted with his kindly expression. He was a peaceful man with twelve children, and now he spoke me as to one of his children. "And because you are a Muslim, you observe the practices of Islam. You're thinking about the process too much. I have seen this before, and there is no end to it. Allah is merciful."

I had reached the end of the discourse. I bowed to the imam, kissed him on the cheek, and departed.

So there was no one I could ask about the level of philosophical certainty I desired. The old imam had done his best, and after I drove home, I settled. Perhaps his answer was the best I had heard. I was adrift.

I kept Talal's word to myself and did not return to the Church of the Holy Ghost and Empty Sepulcher. I told Philip why.

"I understand. Given that you feel this way, you shouldn't go back. You'd be attending on false pretenses. They'd think you're something that you're not. There are other churches in town if you want to see what they have to say. There's one down on Main. They call themselves a Bible church. Their approach is quite different than at the other church."

"Is this like the difference between Sunni and Shia?"

"Yes, I guess it's sort of like that."

The simile pleased me. I would try the other church.

The Open Bible Church was a one-story storefront rented for its weekend use as a church. The service at this church was more reserved, and the preacher's talk followed three points that were at least logical in their progression. The pastor's vocabulary was more varied and precise. A number of attendees were from the university. The people weren't friendly and there were no dinner invitations.

I was free to attend the Open Bible Church without being troubled by messy social invitations and endless, overly friendly greetings. I could sample without being compelled to participate.

I liked the thoughtful approach to explaining the text but there was nothing there that unfolded any level of certainty to me. It was pretty much like Islam in its formulaic approach.

The pastor, as he preached from the letters of Paul, kept referring to the concept of grace, which I couldn't grasp. And his repeated references to Jesus, the dying God, repelled me. I had heard such before, but at the Church of the Holy Ghost and Empty Sepulcher, the descriptions of Jesus' work were joyous. The Open Bible Church was full of intellect and bereft of joy.

I was ready to return to Kuwait.

Chapter 16

The Prodigal Returns and the Lamb is Killed

The long plane flight home was numbing. We stopped for several hours in London, deplaned, woke up a bit, and then got back on the plane almost awake, and I was not fully recovered when the time for the welcome celebration came. I was expected to be bright and outgoing with the guests, and somehow I managed to generate the expected responses.

My family's living conditions had crept into extravagance. They had always been well off, but where there had been adequacy there was now opulence. It was further evident that my father had not been the one responsible for the excess. Salman, never strong during my remembrance, had declined physically and mentally. He was kindly, smiling at my return, but in the background to Suhayb.

The family observed the age-old practice of welcoming home the returning son with a feast featuring the traditionally prepared lamb. Because of the length of the guest list, there were three lambs. Suhayb had spared no expense, particularly in light of the fact this was an opportunity for him to display his own position, in addition to his long absent brother.

The guest list was indeed impressive. There were ministers of various components of the Kuwaiti government and two cabinet members. Emir Abdullah III had been invited but he respectfully declined due to a trip to Bahrain for a meeting with the Khalifa family. The new independent government of Kuwait was rapidly spreading its wings, and there were many decisions in process.

One of these decisions was the role of Sharia law in the legal system. It slowly became clear to me this was issue Suhayb was so carefully orchestrating. Several imams placed themselves in proximity to me and began to make inquiries about my PhD work on the topic. Mainly they were congratulatory and not interested in details. But there was one who was very much interested in the particulars. Suhayb made certain I paid specific attention to Saif al-Din. Saif al-Din was of the same cut as Al-Ghabani, stiff in demeanor, long beard, and short dishdasha, like the Prophet, it was said. There was going to be a challenge of some sort, either frontal or subtler. What did al-Din want from me? After all, I was just a fledging professor at the new university, and I had little interest or intent in politics.

As the close of the evening came nearer, the meal commenced, after which it was the custom that the guests would soon disperse. As they began to eat, Al-Din said softly to me, "Let's talk afterward in the garden."

I obeyed his request, and Suhayb made a point of allowing us to be alone. The evening was warm but now pleasant, and there was a light breeze with no dust in the air. We sat under the large date palm by the fountain. Saif al-Din began, "We're hoping you're just what we need." Who was the 'we' he referred to? "I want you to know we have much to discuss and that we have far to go. The new Emir is interested only in the finances of the country. That's why he's down with the Khalifas. He's strong on money but weak in every other way." *Treasonous conversation.* I blanched at where the conversation might be headed. Saif was quick to sense this response and retreated to more formal discussion.

Saif delicately closed the conversation. "I see you're tired from your travel. Your lips have lost their color. We should talk again soon. And I want to read your thesis and your papers." I was sure his observation about my lips was correct. Saif might actually understand the significance of what the thesis said, and this was only complemented by my subsequent academic contributions, from which conclusions could be drawn if added together in the composite. Could this be potential disaster so soon on my doorstep? How quickly the conflict had developed. Epistemology or reality?

"Yes, by all means. We must talk more."

"May Allah bless you. I will send a message for our next meeting. Good night, my friend."

CHAPTER 17

The Engagement

The next week was spent working through the morass at the new Kuwait University. I expected to sail through the contract process, but the endless paperwork had been given over to mid-level foreign administrators. It was like dealing with the Ottomans. The matter finally came down to a pointless conflict between an Egyptian named Mazin and me. For reasons totally unclear to me, Mazin insisted on sitting on the paperwork, and the appointment therefore couldn't progress. The daily comment from Mazin was *Insha-allah*, or as God wills, meaning in this case that the paperwork could be completed but not likely soon. All that was required was a stamp embossed on the papers. I had decided I would not give a bribe or a "gift." I went home in humiliation.

It was then that Saif al-Din called to set up the meeting. The time was agreed upon, and in passing I mentioned my difficulty at the university.

"That should not be happening."

"Well, I suppose I'll just have to put up with it."

"We will not allow this to continue. What is the name of the one who's the problem?"

Again, there was the "we." "His name is Mazin, in the Faculty Affairs office."

"You should go back on Sunday."

I returned Sunday and went to Mazin's office. His name had been removed from the door, and a young Kuwaiti was sitting at the desk with a large pile of papers strewn out in front of him.

"I'm looking for Mazin."

"He's not here. He's been sent back to Cairo."

I wondered at the course of events that was unfolding. "Mazin was working on my appointment papers."

"Your appointment has been completed. You can pick up the contract down at the end of the hall. They will give you the keys to your office and your teaching assignments."

The stunning reversal seemed somehow connected to my mention of the problem to Saif al-Din. The relevant term in Kuwaiti Arabic is *wasta*, meaning influence from an authoritative source. But the apparent orchestration of events was disturbing in that I did not know where they were leading or who was in charge. I departed from the Faculty Affairs and located my new office, which was cramped, but freshly re-painted.

Two days later I was due at the home of Saif al-Din. The farash led me back to Saif's study. He was a man of letters. The walls were shelved with books, and there were stacks on the desk. A Quran was on the front of the desk with no other books around it or over it. Saif came out from behind the large desk and joined me around a table. The farash delivered tea and shut the door behind him.

"I trust your affairs are now settled at the university."

"Yes, they are now. Thank you for your help."

"We must take care of those who are with us. What we must do is too important to be impeded by shirkers."

My mind reeled with the possibilities. There must be a correct time for questions. But was this the time?

Saif anticipated the question. "You must wonder about the reason for this meeting. Young man, the time is far too vital and the purpose too important to play cat and mouse here." Saif's tone had changed from the kindly old man to one who was in charge. "We must see that Sharia law is installed formally in the government of our new state. And we must insist on the Hanbali school of Sharia."

"What does this have to do with me?"

"Your role is key. You're young. You represent the young people of Kuwait. You've been educated in Great Britain and the US. Your family is well placed by name and influence. Your brother is a leader among us. And there are other reasons which you can probably figure out."

"I'm beginning to understand."

"You know that Al-Ghabani and I were friends." I had not known this. "We have spoken in detail about you. He was very complimentary about your abilities. He did, however, question your priorities." My mind was racing. "It was a terrible thing for the Al-Ghabani family last year."

"Last year?"

"Didn't you know? He shot himself at his home in Jeddah. His blood spilled in front of his family. For a man of his caliber to do such an act against Islam, to commit suicide, it was unbelievable. But considering what happened with him, I suppose I understand. He told me you were responsible for exposing him. This was the only honorable thing you could do. He told us much about you." Saif made eye contact with me.

"I'm sorry for his family." My thoughts gyrated out of control. Did Al-Ghabani disclose the content of the thesis, or even worse, my attendance at the church? Did Saif intend to blackmail me with this information? Was Saif seriously desirous of my input on Sharia law, or was I only a foil in some bigger plan? I didn't trust Saif, and the information about what he wanted was slow in coming out. And Saif kept referring to "we" or "us." Who are they? I couldn't bolt. I had to move along with the plan, whatever it was, at least for now. How could I get out of this? Extraction had become my chosen modus operandi for any conflict.

And on top of the present dilemma was the death of Al-Gha-bani, for which I now felt responsible. This was just another event to add to the long list that had perturbed my conscience from London to the US. I had been able to escape before and now I must do so again.

"What's my role? What do you want from me?"

"Yacoub, I want you to know again there are many among us who consider it vital that Sharia law be installed fully and completely as the law of Kuwait. We don't think there is anything more important. We do not believe any obstacle is fit to stop us. The Emir does not favor this, but..." His voice trailed off as if he did not want to finish the statement. "We want you to know you are part of this process. We know your brother is with us, but we are not yet sure if the degree of his support is sufficient. That's your first job to attend to. There will be other tasks for you."

"I'll speak with Suhayb."

"Yes, I know we can count on you. I expect you to contact me about your conversations with Suhayb. He is an important man now in Kuwait. And by the way, I want to read your thesis."

My approach to Suhayb the next day was cautious. "We must discuss my talks with Saif al-Din."

"Yes, I'm sure you enjoyed him. His interests are much the same as yours. The subtleties of Islam are more in your court."

"I think there's more to it than that. He wants to know where you stand and where your support lies."

"Of course I support him. He is a man of honor and a true Muslim. Why would he need my support?"

"I'm not sure, but it seems he's asking for your support not just for himself but for some group. I have real concerns about what they intend."

"I can't imagine why this question is even being asked. Of course I can support him. I don't see any problem." Suhayb was not a man of subtlety. And perhaps he did not even grasp why his support was required. I knew Suhayb didn't understand where the conservative applications of Sharia would take the country.

Saif was satisfied with my report. It seems he had known Suahyb would not resist and would not fully understand. Now the Al-Tamimi family was engaged in the plan and without full knowledge of its details. I knew now we were being manipulated for some undisclosed purpose, but the next step surprised me.

"Your father will be contacted about a wife for you. Our tribes will be joined by the marriage."

"I'm not ready for marriage. I just got back to Kuwait. I'm not settled."

"A man must have at least one wife." And again the request, "Please get your thesis for me." The connection between the marriage arrangement and the request for the thesis was pointed. Now I knew there was a threat—a threat to reveal the content of my thesis. There were more than academics here. Most would not care or understand about the thesis, but in the hands of those who would understand, it was volatile. And then the final blow, "Dr. Al-Ghabani and I had interesting conversations about your work. There are men in Kuwait who would be interested in its content. I'm sure you understand how important this is for our purpose." The threat had been delivered in full, and I understood.

Three days later Salman informed me the marriage contract had been approved. This was presented as the happy occurrence any young man would relish.

"Yacoub, it is reported to me that Rabea is a beautiful young woman, as her name implies" The name meant "springtime."

The wedding celebration was planned rapidly, and before two weeks elapsed I found myself in the center tent of the men's party. The sword dance where weapons were thrust up and down, with its obvious sexual metaphor, was performed, the expansive meal was served, and the men then carried me out into the desert for a wild ride in a jeep, with celebratory rifle fire.

The wedding itself was brief after the papers were signed. Before that night we had only made brief eye contact. Then, we were alone. The women of both tribes were in the adjoining room making loud ululations. Rabea was thirteen years old, having just reached menarche. We both knew what was expected. I was embarrassed by the girl's youth. Rabea exhibited the degree of virginal resistance that was required by the custom of the desert. After she disrobed, I was shocked to see her breasts had barely begun to fill. Her face was indeed beautiful, but she was a child.

Rabea was frightened, brave and cooperative. I was able to complete the act, and the proof thereof was made available for inspection. At the conclusion of this first encounter, I was filled with remorse, more than even after Anna or Sattie. I was more than twice the age of this child, and I felt I had committed a crime.

Rabea joined the wives in the household of the Al-Tamimi compound. The young girl set about learning the duties of a wife from my mother. We slept together, but I could not bring myself to touch the adolescent Rabea.

The stage was now set for Saif al-Din. I was invited to his home and ushered into the study. Saif was smiling. "I trust you're enjoying your new wife."

"By all means."

"Now that our families are linked, we can speak together as one family." He uncovered several papers and put them in front of me. They were my publications from the US literature recapitulating, in fragmentary form, my thesis work. "I read English very well. It seems we don't need your thesis anymore. Others might not grasp what you've said, but I can explain it to them if it proves necessary. They may be compelled to act against you in your apostasy. You cannot impugn the integrity of the hadiths that are the basis of Sharia. If you help us, however, we will forgive your misadventure. I trust you have secured your brother's cooperation."

"He has agreed." I didn't reveal my brother didn't really understand.

"Good. Now we can proceed. Your brother is a respected imam. Your family name and you as a US-trained professor will give us credibility."

"I know you're serious, but I am not completely sure what's happening."

"Or what's about to happen. Yacoub, we have the opportunity in our new state to install Sharia, the Hanbali School, as the sole basis of our legal system. You will support this in every way we tell you."

"Like the Saudis?'"

"Yes, like the Saudis, but we have the opportunity to carry this out in a more complete and organized fashion."

"As you've said, the Emir does not favor this. I know he's opposed."

"You will hear more about this later. We're publishing our proposal as a letter in the newspaper. All of us, including you and your brother, will sign onto the document."

"May I see the letter?"

"You will see it when it appears in the newspaper."

When Suhayb heard, he was nonplussed. "I've known Saif al-Din since I was a child. He's a man of honor. We shouldn't worry."

"Suhayb, do you really understand what's being proposed? Surely, you know how punishment is meted out in Saudia Arabia."

"You mean they intend to have public severing of hands."

"And heads."

"Allah!"

"And we're to be part of this. There are a number with Saif. I don't know how many."

"We must not be part of this." Suhayb had been naïve.

"Suhayb, we've been manipulated. My marriage to Rabea was part of this. I think they're dangerous. I'm uncertain of their real intent."

CHAPTER 18

Betrayal

The letter appeared in several papers including the *Kuwait Times*, and I was stunned we had been coerced into the fray. Suhayb was beside himself. Even as an imam, he did not support the full implementation of Hanbali Sharia. How had we been forced into such a position? I finally told him about the basis, the thesis and all. Suhayb was an outgoing, charming man, not at all given to subtlety. "Everyone knows how complicated these religious things are. You've studied the hadiths and given your results. I don't see how this brings us to danger. This just doesn't matter to most people."

"Suhayb, these men are dangerous. They've threatened my life in order to secure our participation. There's more to it than religion."

Saif al-Din called a meeting of the group in the basement of his home, and our attendance was expected. We finally encountered the group we were already named a part of. I was frightened. Suhayb remained bewildered. There were conservative imams with views similar to Saif's, but also rich merchants and bank executives. Two were from the Kuwait Oil Company at Ahmadi. The fact there was a heavy representation of financial executives led me to conclude I was correct in my assumption that there was more to the matter than just religious views.

Saif al-Din began, "Gentlemen, our letter has now appeared. They know where we stand. Now, we must put our plan into action. No one is to speak of this outside our group. We know where the Emir stands. He will veto any attempt to install Sharia law in full."

I was unsure how the group would circumvent the Kuwaiti legal system, which was a harmonious mixture of British common law, French and Egyptian civil law, and Islamic law. The complex nature of the system allowed the Emir a considerable measure of control, which he would not surrender.

My puzzlement only increased. At least two-thirds of the men weren't interested in Sharia. Saif al-Din had put together an interesting amalgam, but for what overarching reason? Why would businessmen join with those desiring Sharia?

Saif continued, "We will first approach the Emir as a unified group and present him formally with our proposal. We will make certain the newspapers are present to record our request and his subsequent refusal. The fact that we represent a cross-section of the people will have its impact." Suhayb shook his head at the need for him to appear in such a circumstance.

Sharia was not the sole issue. My mind raced to discern where this was headed.

Saif closed the gathering, "After the meeting with the Emir, we must be ready. Those of you who have the necessary connections, make sure your men are prepared to move. We cannot let the time go by. We must act after the next newspaper report appears. Then, all will know that we act in the interests of Islam in Kuwait."

The real purpose emerged. There was to be a coup to replace the Emir. Saif al-Din and his kind would have their Sharia law, but the others, the merchants, businessmen, and oilmen fitted in, too. They would install their own leadership to gain control of the vast finances of the state. The Kuwait Oil Company was needed for this, as the money was born there.

I explained what was happening to Suhayb, who was in disbelief. He still didn't grasp the danger and seriousness of the plot
until he saw two young men following his children home from
school. Suhayb inquired about their purpose. Their response,
"We are looking after your children in case the plan does not go
well," put Suhayb into a frenzy, and he drove them off in a fury.
He was a strong man. But now he knew the depth of the situation.

His anger spilled out, "Yacoub, what have you gotten us into?
All your expensive education has gotten us this?"

"I know this is my fault, but we've got to stop this plot."

"How do we do that? They've threatened you, and now my
children. Use your devious thoughts to fix this. This will kill our
father. And what's more, our family is dependent on the way the
money flows. We don't want this altered." And so it came down
to this in Suhayb's mind.

"I'll figure it out, just let me think."

The next morning my affliction returned, and the white camel
was there again. Once again, he seemed to appear for my rescue.
Did he bring the solution for good or ill? I awoke and went to the
paper where the letter appeared. The names of the participants
were there, including mine and Suhayb's. The list was invaluable,
but the timing would be critical. I sought out two of my contacts
from the diwaniya, the social group who met weekly for varied
discussions. Khalid and Karam were highly placed in the Kuwaiti
military with ties to the Secret Police. Finally, all my evenings in
the diwaniya as a young man would count for something. I had
been considered a rising star there for my story-telling ability,
and these men thought well of me.

My explanation to the two was lengthy and awkward, but I
scraped through it. The men were astonished that the threat was
so near and well planned. But they relished the idea of saving the
Emir and the honor this would bring them.

The plan was as follows: The traitors would meet with the Emir
about installing Sharia law. Suhayb and I would be there because

we had no choice, and the newspaper would report the event. The coup was to occur immediately after a report sympathetic to the conspirators appeared in the paper. The Sharia issue was only a pretext to power. Therefore, we knew the traitors must be taken into custody simultaneously and before the attempt on the Emir. The plan was just the sort of thing the Secret Police loved. And they would have the element of total surprise on their side.

The day came for the meeting with the Emir. Sabah listened politely to the distinguished group. As predicted, he declined their request for consideration. The next day, the newspaper published the article. As planned, it portrayed the Emir as an enemy of Islam, which he was not, and the group prepared for their coup.

As I designed, the Secret Police rounded up the group at their homes. They were taken handcuffed by bus to the prison, the event shown on TV, and the coup attempt reported in the press. Suhayb and I were briefly heroes for infiltrating the traitors and exposing their plan.

The Emir was beneficent. He did not execute the conspirators. There were twenty-eight of them, and to have done so would have been seen as unduly harsh by the international press. The punishment, however, was both cruel and clever. He confiscated the money and property of the offending families, stripped them of their Kuwaiti citizenship, and exiled them to Saudi Arabia, all with the blessing of King Faisal. Faisal had the state machinery in place to handle those with Wahhabi leanings and more experience in maintaining the upper hand in such situations.

My household driver took Rabea to the home of Saif al-Din to say good-bye to her parents. She returned after several hours, and I saw she concealed something under her abaya, an object that was nearly too heavy for her.

"Do you need help?"

"No, it's nothing." She hastened to the bedroom. Clearly it was more than "nothing."

"Rabea, let me see what you've brought back." Rabea decided it was pointless to deny, and she brought out from under her the abaya a large teak wood box.

I opened the clasp on the box, which disclosed all manner of gold bracelets and necklaces, cramped tightly to the brim of the box. "Rabea, what have you done?"

"I've taken my mother's gold."

"How could you do this?"

"They traded me like a camel. I'm thankful to Allah they traded me to a kind man like you, but it could have been otherwise. Now, I have collected my own bride price."

Another reason to reassess my young wife. But again the camel came in the morning. He told me he didn't like Rabea.

The traitors and their immediate families were relegated to the area south of the Empty Quarter near the Yemeni border. Would they ever again be a threat?

I secured the thesis from my packed belongings and asked the new librarian to file it in the Kuwait University Library. The leather-bound dissertation would become dusty and remain unread for many years.

* * *

As a result of an episode of sleep paralysis, I arrived late at the diwaniya, and the topic of the evening was the subject of a recent sermon from Friday prayer. The imam had enunciated the primacy of Islam to the point of the destruction of other religions. The men of the diwaniya were not normally interested in such talks but the vigorous tone of the imam's sermon was troubling to all, and now this came on the heels of the near coup. Kuwait had tolerated the views of others for many years, and many expatriot workers were Christian.

The discussion went on for some time, and I took a position on theoretical grounds that questioned Sharia law. Professor Al-

Bader from the philosophy department accosted me as we left the diwaniya. He saw where my thoughts were headed. "Why do you persist in subterfuge? I know where this business about *fiqh* is headed. I know what you've said in your papers. Sometimes I think you're an enemy of Islam from reading them. I would tell your father, or the others, but they wouldn't get it." He wasn't angry, but concerned.

At that moment several others joined us, and the difficult conversation was over before it began.

CHAPTER 19

Rabea

Everyone in the family was aware Rabea had some involvement in Saif's plot, if only as a pawn. It was evident that the marriage had been secured under false pretenses, or as Rabea said, a camel trade. Saif al-Din considered her to be chattel, and it was the design of her life as an uneducated woman.

Under this sort of scrutiny from the family and the potential dislike and distrust, I observed that Rabea gained the family's admiration for her toughness and quiet persistence. She remained civil and congenial in the face of the difficult situation that had been created by the recent political events. Rabea never argued but did not retreat.

With all the high-tension events and added complexities at the university, I was mentally and physically exhausted. In addition, to my embarrassment, I told Rabea I had been falling asleep during my classes as the students were speaking.

As we were preparing for sleep late in the evening, Rabea said, "There is something I want to ask you." I feared she was going to inquire about the performance of my marital duties. I wasn't ready yet. "Yacoub, I want to learn to read." I was blind-sided by the request. The idea that this unsophisticated Bedouin girl would want to read would never have occurred to me. I had lived the West for ten years and was quite aware that Western women had the same desires, but I had not made the transition to my own culture. I briefly experienced guilt at my lack of insight.

"Yes, of course. We can do this in the evenings." The next morning I rummaged through the schoolbooks I had used as a child and put them in our bedroom.

I didn't know how to approach the teaching of reading, but I did my best. First, I began with the alphabet and the sounds the letters generated. This effort was Rabea's assignment until she mastered them. She stole away from next day's work when she could, so that her studying would be in secret.

I couldn't believe how quickly she learned. I had rarely encountered this level of mental quickness and never among my Kuwaiti male colleagues. She learned the letters and sounds individually and rapidly moved to changing the beginnings and endings of words as they were placed in context. She was soon reading texts, slowly but accurately, and her speed improved. She then asked for a dictionary. I had never seen a student devour a dictionary, but there it was.

The time we spent at night alone in or bedroom increased, and my admiration for the young girl intensified. Rabea's appetite for reading was not confined to any particular subject matter. Anything I brought home for her was consumed, after which she wanted to discuss the content. In the evenings she exhausted me with her interrogations. She seized new information and strangled the life out of it. Her ability to synthesize ideas challenged my own, something no one else had been able to achieve. Seeing our time alone in the evenings, Salman commented, "Soon I will have another grandson." But there would be none for some time, at least none that he knew about.

At the university I received a letter from the US. The postmark was from Tucson, and there was no return address. Inside the envelope was a photograph of a little boy with dark eyes, black curly hair, and delicate features. I tore the envelope into small pieces so that the postmark would not be recognizable, and put the photo into the top desk drawer. I didn't want the photo at home where it might elicit a question from Rabea.

While the hours Rabea and I spent alone in the evenings were a joy, the passage of the time without the production of offspring was an increasing concern for the family. The lack of a pregnancy with so much time alone together was taken as a signal of infertility. And of the two of us, of course, Rabea was the one to receive the blame. Even Fatima, who had been Rabea's supporter, began to push for an alternative. The alternative was a second wife, one who was proven in bearing children.

I learned of the developing plan. While we were not yet living fully as man and wife, my love for Rabea had grown. Though I was free to take a second wife and it was often done when there was no offspring after a time, I was saddened by the possibility and the knowledge there was nothing I could do to stop it. I was distraught by my own passivity in the matter. Not only would I see less of Rabea, our evening sessions over reading material would be truncated. I resolved to get more books so she could proceed on her own. She was far enough along now to be independent in her learning.

CHAPTER 20

Another Wife

Suhayb took charge of the wife-finding. He used his contacts among the Islamic community to ensure that the choice would be honorable and in keeping with his own views. Among the Al-Murra tribe he located a woman of twenty-eight, recently divorced, but with two small children, thus demonstrating that she was not barren. One of the Al-Murra tribal leaders, Malik, proposed the match.

Huda was tall, firmly built and devoid of cheer. I had no reason to veto the match, and the arrangements proceeded. Since the two children were quite young, they would reside in the Al-Tamimi household until such time as the father chose to take them. The Al-Tamimi compound, due to the success of Suhayb's strong management skills, was ample and could easily accommodate the additional family. I would now have two families, but the relationship between the two wives was immediately awkward. Rabea was the first and therefore the senior wife. Huda, however, was older and larger physically, to the point of being intimidating. She was cold to Rabea, who was willing to comply with the arrangement. The silent agreement was that they would avoid each other.

By obligation my nights were divided between the woman and the girl. I fulfilled my physical duties with Huda. She was sexually experienced, and made the duty easy. Within three months she was pregnant. Rabea pressed my mind to its limits. Her interests did not know any boundary. Whatever was in print she wanted to know about, why such and such line of reasoning was taken, why a particular word was chosen, always some probing question. How could Rabea be so tolerant of the dual arrangement?

At first, the two women in the household were not a problem for me. I took delicious pleasure in the alternating variety: the sexual storm on one night followed by the intellectual stretch on the following night. And Rabea extended the bounds of my own intellect. Huda's pregnancy developed and after a time, sexual intercourse became inconvenient, resulting in more time with Rabea and her reading and thinking adventures.

The birth of Huda's baby was an event of mixed results. I was the proud father of a son, Thawab. Thawab's arrival, however, spawned conflict within the household. Suhayb raised concerns about my continuing loyalty to Rabea over the more productive Huda. "Why do you remain loyal to that little girl? She's not fit to be the senior wife. Maybe it would be better if you simply divorced her." Salman was passive about the matter. Fatima was still a supporter of Rabea. And so it went.

As this family squabble persisted, Rabea pursued her education quietly. The Filipino maid, Divina, supplemented Rabea's schooling with an Arabic translation of the New Testament. The maid couldn't read Arabic but she knew the English version well. She had purchased the Arabic version at one of the bookstores in town especially for Rabea, whom she loved dearly. Of course, Rabea would read anything. The next few months for Rabea were a quest the likes of which I had not observed. She was desirous of information simply for the information itself, a true learner. The New Testament provoked all kinds of questions that I couldn't answer. Rabea was often critical of the text. She was particularly offended by the first verse of the Gospel of Mark: "The beginning of the gospel of Jesus Christ, the son of God."

"Yacoub, how can this be? This Bible is a book read by many over the world. Yet here is a lie. God cannot have a son. It's completely ridiculous in every way. Why is this statement so clear in this book? Is Mark trying to offend the reader?"

"I don't know. I haven't read the book. It sounds like it might be dangerous for you to read it. Maybe you should move on to something else."

"But why do so many read it? And Islam speaks favorably of the people of the book, as they are called. My mother used to say this before my father silenced her."

"Some of the Christians in the US seemed very happy with their beliefs. Their beliefs seemed almost magical to me—not based on what seemed reasonable."

"And I read about the Christians consuming the body of God, and, as they say, being 'filled'with the Holy Ghost. This is as peculiar as God having a son!"

"I can't help you. I think you should put the book away."

I heard nothing more of the book for some time. We had tacitly agreed not to discuss it.

The next evidence of the effect of the book occurred after Rabea carelessly left the New Testament in one the rooms frequented by others. The book was brought to Suhayb who was beside himself. He broke the basic rules and interrogated Rabea, which I learned of after the fact.

"Where did you get this?"

"I don't wish to tell you."

"Was it from Yacoub?"

"No."

"Then, where did you get it?"

Her desire was to protect me. Finally she had to confess that the maid, Divina, had given it to her.

The issue then developed into an argument between Suhayb and me. After all, Suhayb had convened a disciplinary conversation with Rabea without my knowledge.

Divina was taken to the airport and flown back to the Philippines, where she would be required to remain until such time as Suhayb might allow her return. She had been the only support for her family, and Rabea was filled with guilt at what she had done. I failed in my support. "I told you to get rid of the book. Now see what you've done."

Weeks passed before Rabea resumed her reading adventures, but she couldn't resist any longer.

"Yacoub, I want you to get some more reading material for me."

"What do you have in mind?"

"The book Divina gave me—it was called the New Testament. So, if there is a new testament, there must be an old testament. And the book often referred to a text from an older source. Can you get it for me?"

"Haven't we had enough trouble with this?

"I'll be more careful this time, I promise."

I did as my young wife asked. I was familiar from my US time that such a book did exist, though it had not received much attention in the two churches I had visited. I was unable to locate an Old Testament in Arabic.

"Rabea, the only copy of the Old Testament I can find is in English."

"Where is it?'

"I said it's in English. What's the point of getting it for you?"

"I need to learn English anyway." Again, there was this stubborn desire directed at learning something. Perhaps she needed more household assignments. "Yacoub, I know they teach English as a course at the university. Please get me the Bible book and the textbooks on English. I can learn it myself. I don't need you to teach me." And she didn't.

Within six months she was reading the Old Testament in English. I read some of it, too, to see what she found so interesting. I found long lists of old names, some reminiscent of the Arabic, and endless tales of battles between warring tribes. My interest was not piqued, even when she pointed out my biblical namesake, Jacob, as it is spelled in the English Bible. "Yacoub, he is so like you. He is the one who grasps, the one who reaches for the heel of the other. He had strange experiences in sleep, just as you do. And he is a story-teller."

"I know about the ladder and the angels and about the wrestling match by the stream. I agree these are beautiful pictures but they are only a recitation of dreams or someone's imagination."

But Rabea was enthralled, and I heard her pray I would take an interest in the text.

She also prayed for a replacement copy of the New Testament, too, but her recall of the confiscated text was still well preserved.

"Yacoub, we need to talk more. I know you've been avoiding any discussion with me. Even so, I greatly enjoy your company even when we don't talk about anything other than the events of the day. But this is important. It's about the book."

"Alright, let's talk." I was afraid this was going to come up again. Rabea had been much too involved with the old book. Better to have this conversation in private than to have it arise openly in the family.

"Yacoub, I believe this book is true. I want you to know this, too."

"What in the world do you mean, true? The Quran has surpassed everything there is in the old book. Perhaps there are some things that are accurate, but to say the book is true—that's apostasy by any measure. You can't let anyone hear you say that. Maybe I don't understand what you mean."

"Yacoub, what I mean is that the contents of the book, both books really, from beginning to end, force me to believe."

"Believe? How can you believe without knowing for certain it's true? And there is no way you can know that. I've attempted the same with Islam so that I could know, for certain, the truth. What is it, exactly, that you believe?"

"I know you're going to be shocked. I don't want that. I don't want it to separate us and what we have together."

"We've come this far. Let's get on with it."

"Yacoub, I believe that God has a son, as Mark said. Everything in both books points to this."

"That's heresy."

"That's not all. I believe this son is also God himself. And I believe that son, the son who is God, was killed for me."

I couldn't continue with the conversation, and Rabea must know I couldn't absorb any more blows. She stroked my hair.

"You must not speak of this to any one else."

"I understand." And she kept the confidence.

I didn't sleep at all in the early part of the night. Rabea slept soundly. In the morning, I once again found myself awake but unable to move. I expected the white camel would come, but no camel. I had set out in his studies as a young man thinking that, with enough knowledge and learning, I would be able to know the truth in an absolute way. I had failed. Was I farther from knowing? Here I lay beside this early figure of a woman, still really a girl. And now she had uttered this belief, not knowledge, but belief. The idea of belief, rather than precise knowledge as an endpoint, had not entered my mind. Is it possible I would remain stuck in this impasse for the rest of my life?

CHAPTER 21

A New Friend

In 1969 John Freidecker came to the university as a faculty member in the Department of History. He was then the only American in the Arts Faculty. His special area of expertise was the history of economic development. I missed Americans and befriended John, who was anxious to know Kuwaitis.

John was a fisherman, tanned and with skin toughened from years on the water, and I took him out near Failaka Island to fish for hamour. Our trip was a success with several large fish, and the evening being pleasant with a light breeze, we barbecued them over a charcoal fire. The beach along the Failiaka coast wasn't hospitable but we found a large flat rock near the sea. The hamour were flaky and white. We ate every scrap and laid back looking upward. We were far from the lights of the city, and the sky over the island was as the sky over the desert at night. John had never seen the stars with such clarity.

I sketched out the history of the island. "We believe the human history of Failaka goes back at least as far as the Dilmun era." John, as a historian himself, was familiar with Dilmun and the development of that culture near present-day Bahrain. "There were continuous settlements here on the island as a shipping port along the route from the Far East to the areas north of here. Alexander the Great and the Greeks were here for a time.

Alexander called the island Icarus. And we think several of the ruins represent Christian churches, perhaps a gift from Egypt. All this predated Islam. Much of the area's pre-Islamic history is likely preserved here, if we were to dig deep enough. There's more below the Islamic soil than on top of it."

The fire had gone out.

I continued, "I envy the Dilmunites."

"How's that? That's a strange comment. Why in the world do you envy them? We don't even know who they were."

"I don't know why I feel that way. I think it's because they were closer to creation." My comment, I thought, fit with the starry sky. "The knowledge of the world then was fresh. We've diluted it all, to its detriment."

"What do you think they had?"

"Of course I really don't know, but there're remnants. There are the epics or myths. Gilgamesh is one that students like, and it's related to Dilmun. The flood story and all that."

Finally John asked, "How do you think the myths stack up?"

"There must be some thread of truth under them. Why else would they be composed?"

John stated his view. "I always thought they arose from hopes and dreams."

"But there are physical remnants that are left. There are the artifacts here on Failaka that aren't even identified. Some have suggested the Garden of Eden was here. On Bahrain there's a tree out in the middle of the desert called the Tree of Life. They say it's only four hundred hundred years old, but someone had the idea very long ago. And then there are the mysterious burial mounds on the island. Up north of here in Iraq in the little town of Al-Qurnah, there's another Tree of Life. I saw it years ago. The tree's dead but the inhabitants built a memorial of sorts around it. It must mean something to them. I think the Dilmunites were aware of something we're not. All three of these places have been identified with the Garden, though now it's sort of a cruel joke."

John asked, "What does the Quran say about the tree?"

"The details are thin, but they were instructed not to approach the tree."

"No more details about the tree?'

"No."

John continued, "In Genesis there were many trees but there are two mentioned by name."

"Two trees instead of one?'

"Yes, one is the Tree of Life."

"And that's the one that they say is around today."

"I guess you could say that."

"What about the second tree?"

"That's the Tree of the Knowledge of Good and Evil. That's the one they weren't supposed to eat."

"And that's the tree that's not around today?"

"Nope," said John.

"That's what I was afraid of. That's just my point."

We got back into the boat and motored back to the city. We were quiet because it was late.

* * *

I brought John to the next diwaniya as a guest. John could grasp a bit of the Arabic, enough to recognize the conversation was an odd continuation of our Failaka exchange.

I had hoped to provoke discussion on the hadiths, as this had been the subject of my thesis and the pursuit of my academic life. I failed. The diwaniya wouldn't touch the issue.

As I drove him back to his home, John questioned. "Why did you challenge the group with your odd story about the hadiths? What was the point? There might be some there who would care about what you said."

"I don't know why I went that direction. It was foolish, wasn't it? Sometimes the stories just come out."

By this time we had reached John's villa. As he got out of the car, he smiled and said, "I think there's more to it than that."

CHAPTER 22

The Great Divorce

When I arrived back at the family compound, I was tired from the diwaniya and its need to maintain those relationships. I wanted only to go to bed. I wished it was Rabea's turn for the evening, as further effort would not be required of me, but it was Huda's and more would be expected.

But I was greeted by both women, still up, dressed, and in the kitchen. They weren't making tea. I had not heard Rabea express herself so forcefully. Should I intervene? I did not immediately grasp the point of the argument, and I let things go too far. They were fighting over my presence at night in the bedroom.

"Don't ever forget that I am the first wife," Rabea asserted.

"You may be the first but you've not proved yourself as a wife. You've not conceived a child. The servants say you don't try." How did the servants know? The failure of Rabea to conceive was my responsibility entirely.

"You're a cruel woman who already failed in one marriage even though you had two children for your first husband." How could Rabea be so harsh? Yet I was pleased by her defense of our relationship, as incomplete as it was.

"There's no point in wasting Yacoub's nights in your bed. He should be in mine every night. I know what to do with a man, and you don't. That's the way we'll settle this. I'm older and stronger than you. I am, in fact, the senior wife."

"I won't have this discussion with you!"

"We're having this discussion, and Yacoub is going to agree with me in order to have more sons. You'll see—isn't that the way it should be, Yacoub?" Huda pushed me for an answer.

I was mute.

"This gentle man cannot be forced to respond."

At that point Huda picked up the iron pan she had been holding and struck Rabea on the side of her head. The sudden loud sound elicited my collapse into a heap alongside Rabea.

Suhayb entered the kitchen and defused the altercation with his physically imposing presence. "Everyone is to retire—right away—now. Yacoub, I think it's best for you to sleep in the other side of the compound tonight." Yes, definitely.

Morning and breakfast came and the three of us, Rabea and Huda and me, did not speak to one another. I went to the university to teach, leaving Rabea and Huda to settle the argument.

By my return there was no evidence that the women had spoken, and the evening stretched before me with certain conflict. In terms of the timing of my spending the night with one of my wives, I had missed the rotation with Huda and it was Rabea's turn. I must make a choice.

I had thought about the choice all day and by the time of my arrival to home, there really was no choice to be made. I loved Rabea. At the time of our marriage she was just a girl foisted upon my family and me for political purposes. But she had matured quickly and her intellect had announced itself. Her figure was full now and there was no longer the apprehension of a sexual relationship with a child. Rabea was a match. My return to our bedroom that night was the physical seal for our marriage. And the next morning, the camel was furious at what I had done. Why did the camel care? Could a dream camel bite?

For Huda, this was the seal of the end of our union. She had seen this coming and had constructed the conflict from desperation. She knew her contribution of the son to the marriage was her only asset, so she chose to emphasize this fact by stealing the marital bed, and the gambit had failed. She packed, gathered her three children, and left for her father's house.

Suhayb was furious. "Yacoub, you must go get her. We cannot allow this. She has borne your only son."

But Thawab was not my only son. "Let her go. It's for the best. She has done what you wanted."

"I insist you fetch her. I'll go with you to effect the reconciliation."

"There will be no reconciling. You saw her strike Rabea."

"Forget that stick of a girl. She's here only because you went too deep in your studies. I don't know what you conceived in your study of Sharia, but it must have been terrible, an apostasy."

"I love Rabea."

"What does that have to do with it?" Your own father manages two wives, one he loves and one he does not.

"Suhayb, I'm finished with this."

"No, we're not finished. I staked my reputation as an imam on this. It's important to our business and to the mosque."

"Is there any difference between the mosque and the business?"

Suhayb ignored the comment. "We'll see what our father has to say."

He presented the conflict to Salman, but the old man was long past settling matters of business or heart.

I would not allow reconciliation, and I learned only later what Suhayb had arranged. He located another mate for Huda. He explained the settlement, "You will be pleased to know that you're rid of her. She will be married to our cousin. He needs a wife to bear him a son, and we know she possesses that skill. The marriage, it was agreed, will occur after a required period of three months to make sure she's not pregnant with your child. You are not to share a bed with her again." My shoulders relaxed.

"There is another part of the settlement. We have agreed you will give them your skill."

"What do you mean?"

"The Emir has created a committee to study how to implement Sharia into our court system. As one who has studied Sharia, we have agreed you will serve as a faithful, knowledgeable Muslim. We can prepare the damage done to the community by Saif. Malik, who arranged your marriage to Huda, is the chairman of the new committee."

"What do you mean, 'We have agreed?' You are not my agent."

"In this matter, I am."

"I don't have time. I can't do this."

"You'll do it. It's our family's honor at stake."

I was trapped again in Sharia. I had pursued Sharia so I could know the truth of it. Instead I found a confusing morass of textual data that had confounded knowing. Here I was again at a personal stalemate. Would this ever end?

Instead of exploding over the imposed predicament, I drifted off into a deep sleep.

When I awoke, I was alone, and the room was dark.

"

CHAPTER 23

Another Committee

The committee convened, and I found myself to be the principal member. How odd, since I was no longer sure what I believed. The meeting took place in the diwaniya room of the Al-Ghazali family of the Al-Murra tribe, who had bargained the marriage for Huda. The group was not totally fundamentalist in character by any means. The Emir had chosen the group wisely, and it was evident from its composition that he intended nothing to arise from it. I was therefore relieved that there would be little pressure to produce a conclusion. Still there was my personal confusion over Sharia and the need to conceal this from the others.

The senior member of the Al-Ghazali family, Malik, opened the meeting, and he singled me out.

"Yacoub, as you are the one who has studied Sharia with an American academic degree, we would like you to record our actions and transmit them to the Emir." My disavowal of the marriage to Huda had put me in this position. "The Emir expects we will report at least every two months. Now I would like the members to introduce themselves." The two-month interval, I was confident, could easily be translated into six.

Introductions proceeded interminably. Most were present for reasons unknown to me. They were in various businesses and had no skill in law of any kind, let alone in Sharia. One, Dirar, was a little-known imam. Another was a cousin of the Emir. And as such he was probably the key figure to observe and please. Only two could be described as knowledgeable and even interested in Sharia. One stated his view as Salafist and the other as Hanbali. If this could be considered balance, then so it was.

Malik laid out his ideas for an agenda. "First we must make our choices about the sources for our study. Then, we will discuss the various levels of law to be undertaken. Finally, using the material at hand we will write the specifics of the code."

It was clear to me that Malik had no idea about the enormity of the task or even what the "sources" were.

One of the businessmen interjected, "I think we must first decide whether this should be done at all." There was murmuring within group, and I couldn't guess what the overall view was, or even if there was one. Most Kuwaitis conveniently professed Islam, but they considered it an impediment to their social life and, in general, to the life of their country.

If my own view ever came out, I could be condemned as an apostate.

CHAPTER 24

Now the Committee is Glorious

The committee came to be called, grandiosely, The Emir's Glorious Committee of the Holy Sharia. The gift of a high-sounding title was the guarantee of minimal expectations. The statement made by the title would be sufficient to bare the weight of the result or, more likely, the lack thereof. I had never before heard the word "Holy" attached to Sharia, but reserved only for the Quran.

The committee rapidly evolved to a diwaniya at Malik's home, so this became more a social commitment rather than anything else. This tied up two evenings a week as I was expected also at Abu Hassan's diwaniya. But the major disadvantage of the new diwaniya was that it kept the albatross of Sharia around my neck in a regularly recurring fashion. And there was always the risk that my real views of Sharia and the hadiths would be revealed. Given the composition of the committee, however, there was little actual chance of dangerously probing questions. I could mask my thoughts without challenge from any of them.

With this undercurrent always present, I was occasionally asked to give technical presentations of various aspects of Sharia. Most of these were easy and too complex for the others to integrate into any sort of indictment.

Juxtaposed with Sharia were my conversations with John Friedecker. John was now settled in with his family and more comfortable with Kuwait. He appeared to enjoy the evolving conversations with me, which covered an ever-widening range of topics, but somehow centered on religion. As a student of history, John lapped up my knowledge of the Middle East. He was a Christian, but he appeared to have little interest in pushing his view. John with his family was attending the National Evangelical Church of Kuwait (NECK).

One evening as we strolled down by the Gulf on the seaside of Gulf Road, I filled in John on the history of the NECK.

"The church compound you see across the street has been there for more than fifty years."

John still had not yet assimilated the idea of Christianity existing alongside Islam in an Islamic state. "How have they persisted so long?"

"The Reformed Church of America first sent a mission to Kuwait about 1900. I don't know what they were reformed from."

John smiled, "That's a good question."

"Anyway, they set up shop to sell Bibles shortly after that and the land you see across the street was purchased by the mission in 1910. Today, such a purchase wouldn't be allowed. They began hospital services in 1914, first with a men's hospital."

"First things first."

"And then with a women's hospital in 1920. In 1931 a church was built on the property. The teak wood trim was brought from India. Gradually several congregations were added according to the tastes of the various ex-patriot groups who were Christians."

"There's no hospital anymore?"

"The hospital was closed a few years ago, in 1967. There are plenty of them around Kuwait now. There's no longer any need. Oil is the miracle drug of the day."

"The NECK seems to exist under some sort of privilege in Kuwait. I didn't think we would find a church in Kuwait."

"The privilege is based on its history. The story is that some sons of the royal family were born in the hospital. Believe it or not, our constitution guarantees freedom of religion."

"What about for you—are you free?"

"I'm free to remain a Muslim."

"What would happen if you went to the NECK?"

"Well, I have no intention of doing that."

"But what if you did?"

"I'd hate to think. It would destroy my family. I suppose I could be killed, perhaps by my own family as a matter of honor."

"Since I've been in Kuwait, I've heard the word 'honor' a lot."

"That's really all there is for us."

"But what about your honor personally, being true to yourself, that sort of thing?"

"I hadn't thought of it like that. I guess you could say it doesn't exist here. We don't deal with the concept of honor on a personal basis. It's a matter of family."

As they were sitting on the beach, I became silent for a time. Finally, it dawned on John that I was actually asleep. I had gone to sleep in the midst of the conversation. John let this pass for a few minutes, but then nudged me.

"I've noticed you do that periodically. Don't you sleep at night?"

"Yes, I sleep well until early morning, but I just can't keep from falling asleep like that."

"Well, I hope it's not a problem for you."

My thoughts went back to the little boy I struck and killed when I went to sleep while driving. I lied. "No, it's not a problem."

"You mentioned the constitution. What else does it say about Islam?"

"It states Sharia is the main basis of our legislation."

"What does that mean?"

"It means whatever we want it to mean." And then in a single moment Sharia and my commission of manslaughter came to mind.

"I don't know what Sharia is."

"I'll try to put together an explanation for you. That'll force me to think about it logically, and I'm sorry to say it's not arranged in any simple way. Otherwise it's pretty hopeless to speak of it to a Westerner without my presenting it in a clear manner."

"I'll look forward to that."

We rose from the beach and took off our sandals and socks. John rolled up his trousers, and I hiked up my dishdasha. The evening was warm and the water was near the same temperature. There were boats returning from fishing, and we looked over the catch, reminding us of our day on Failaka. We promised each other to go out again soon.

John began, "Seeing this, I get the feel of why fishing was such a prominent part of the Bible."

"Really, I hadn't thought about that way. That makes it sound more like a story."

"A story is what it is." John didn't offer to explain.

"You know, I went to church a few times in the US."

"What did you think?"

"It was confusing to me—didn't really make sense. There was all that about the father, son and Holy Ghost—it was a mystery to me."

"You're right again. It's a mystery."

"Then I understand there's a verse that calls Jesus the Son of God. Of course that's just not possible." I didn't mention this was the verse that had challenged Rabea.

"You've had philosophy and logic courses. You know you can't say something is not possible just because you don't know it or believe it."

"But it involves the idea of generation of another person by God."

"That's not the idea at all." John was getting tired of the conversation, and he speeded up his gait to reach his car.

But I wasn't finished. "One of the preachers actually said God would give you anything you asked for. I've never seen or heard of that being true, not for anyone. It's just ridiculous."

"I think the passage he's referring to is from Matthew. There's a lot more to it. If you were a little boy and you asked your mom for a snake, would she give it to you?" John was ready to go home and see his family. He smiled, promised further talks and got into his car.

I drove home feeling I had wasted the evening with John and gotten no answers. He knew more than he was telling. Perhaps John knew I could get answers from someone else, but I was reluctant to tackle the questions with Rabea. She frightened me with her new beliefs and confidence. And here again Sharia was staring me down. *I won't think about either—not Christianity, not Sharia.*

But I couldn't think about anything else. The next morning I awoke and once more found myself paralyzed. I expected the white camel to appear and deliver me in some white camel way. But the dreamland was vacant. Perhaps he had deserted me in anger. The paralysis departed and I went to the university. As my questions multiplied, I was scheduled to teach a class on Sharia law, this time to third year students. The preparation for the class helped me organize my thoughts for John. *A catharsis in the making?*

CHAPTER 25

Committee Action and Sharia

The glorious committee proceeded. There, any sense of attacking the problem was inconceivable, and I was grateful. Two members of the committee diwaniya debated their views. The Salafist emphasized the strict importance of the Sunnah, or the way of the Prophet, with the sideline of maintaining a dishdasha above the ankles. The Hanbali advocate tried valiantly to differentiate himself from the Salafist but in reality there was little difference. Al-Ghabani, of course, was Hanbali, a fact I well recalled. Six months passed in this manner, and there was no pressure from the Emir for a conclusion. Malik reported to the Emir we were making great progress, and this met the full requirement. I longed for it to be over. It would never be over. The two main issues to be dealt with, the sources of Sharia and their implementation in Kuwaiti life, still lurked in the diwaniya's coffee and tea.

* * *

April 1971 and my mind wandered during the long Friday sermon at the mosque. The sermon dealt with the vitality of God's law. It was confusing and lacking in the necessary clarity of argument. I used the time to compose explanation of Sharia for John.

John and I motored out to Failaka. The temperature was already well into the nineties and the humidity surprisingly high. The 25-horsepower Evinrude overheated in the bath-like water, and I shut down the motor for a time to let it cool. We drifted, subject to the breeze and gentle current. The sea was green, and the waves rocked boat. As we began to converse, I drifted off to sleep without warning.

John allowed me to sleep, went to back of the boat, and restarted the motor. I roused with the sound the engine, and we proceeded to the proximity of the island, where we anchored. We baited our lines and began to fish.

"Yacoub, I've noted you seem to go to sleep easily and without warning. Are you okay?"

"Oh, I'm fine, I've done that for years. It's never been a problem."

"What about when you're driving?"

"It's never happened when I'm driving." I lied again.

"Maybe there's some type of medicine that might help."

"I think I'm adjusted to it."

Just then a large hamour took John's line. He brought in the fish, netted it, and put it in the cooler.

"You were going to tell me about Sharia."

"I guess I've been putting it off."

"Why's that? Everyone at the school says you're the expert. I'm starting to feel you have an aversion to the topic."

"It's not an easy subject. It's hard to organize. When I first began to learn about Sharia I thought I'd know the truth about the law. I was naïve."

"I'll forgive any lack of precision."

"Sharia is an old word that means the path to the watering hole."

"I can see how that usage came about in the desert. It's a beautiful idea."

"It should have stopped there. The sources of Sharia are the Quran, of course, as the primary source, and the Sunnah, which is a combination of various elements that are essentially Islamic tradition. The foundations of the Sunnah are the hadiths, which are sayings and practices of the Prophet."

"How many hadiths are there?"

"Thousands. I don't think anybody knows for certain. There are sources that give definite numbers, but they don't agree. There are actually many sets or collections of hadiths. And of course there's overlap among the sets. The classical one is the *Sahih Al-Bukhari*. That's the one I did my PhD thesis on."

"How do you know what is a hadith and what isn't?'

"It has to do with the documentation of the transmission of the hadith from the first observer or listener in company of the Prophet and then through the subsequent transmitters. It's like a pedigree. The first transmissions were verbal."

"I'm trying not be critical but..."

"Go ahead."

"It sounds like there's room for error."

"When I first started down this trail, I hoped not, but you're right. Anyway, there is the Quran and the Sunnah with the hadiths. This is the source of Sharia."

"Doesn't sound too bad."

"And then there's *fiqh*, which is human reason imposed on the Quran and Sunnah."

"Always gets us into trouble, doesn't it."

"That's more or less where the various schools of Sharia come into the picture."

"And how many of those are there?"

"How many Muslims are there on Earth?"

"So what's this grand committee you're on?

"Not grand, it's glorious. The slower the committee works the better. I'm afraid where it might lead and that, at some point, I might have to say what I really think."

"How would Sharia actually work?

"The worry, my worry, is that it could become the basis for law in Kuwait. And that would be all kinds of law—criminal, civil, personal life. Right now the role of Sharia is limited. That's the way the Emir wants it. He's a sharp politician, and he knows the creation of a committee is the surest way to block progress."

A fish took my bait and nearly tore the rod from my hands. My foot kicked the tackle box and the loud sound provoked one of my falling spells. John grabbed the rod before it disappeared into the depths and landed the fish.

"What happened to you?"

"It's happened before—usually when I'm surprised like that."

"I really think you should have it all checked. There's an American doctor I know, a neurologist, coming to Kuwait for a visit. He's a professor in the US. I could ask if he would see you."

The two fish were our only catch, and I gave them to John for his family.

"I guess there's no problem in seeing him—but it's just the way I am."

CHAPTER 26

Am I Insane?

The visit of Professor Alden Alsop was sponsored by the Ministry of Health to bolster Kuwait's medical specialty system, with Alsop in the area of neurology. The Ministry had booked Alsop for a number of conferences and lectures, which were to take place over the second week of October 1971. Alsop was an expert in disorders episodically manifesting themselves in behavior, such as psychomotor seizures.

John informed me he and Alsop had known each other in the States through mutual acquaintances, and he arranged the connection as Alsop stayed at the International Hotel. The three of us first had dinner together at the hotel.

I wore the traditional white dishdasha, and as a well-known scholar of a prominent family, we received privileged service. The conversation turned to Islam. Alsop knew little about the religion, as was the case for most Westerners of the time. Alsop began, "I bought a copy of the Quran at a bookstore the first of the week. I've had some trouble getting into it."

I went to the basics in a gentle way. "First, and I know this sounds strange or perhaps impolite, you didn't buy a copy of the Quran. The Quran itself is only in Arabic. The precision of the primary language is intrinsic to the message. So you bought a translation of the Quran. And the text itself is confusing for a

Westerner. It's arranged roughly from the longest to the short-est chapter, but in fact Mohammed specified the order. It's not chronological either."

Alsop continued, "The second chapter was 'The Red Heifer.' What's the reason for that title?"

"That refers to one of the Hebrew animals of sacrifice in the Old Testament. There's a link between the Quran and the Bible, but it's far from a one-to-one relationship."

"And I noticed there were verses that seemed contradictory. Some were very forgiving to non-Muslims and others were con-demning and even threatening."

"You've hit on a trouble spot. The milder verses were the earlier ones, when Mohammed was in Mecca. The more diffi-cult verses were from Medina. And the text is not linear in this regard."

"Which ones count?"

"There's not a simple answer. God has a right to clarify or replace his own word. Some call it the principle of abrogation, meaning the later verses replace the earlier. But both count."

Alsop responded, "That doesn't seem consistent with revela-tion. But one thing for sure, you can't argue with God. The New Testament of the Bible might be said to abrogate the old, with regard to the ceremonial law."

"At least you're willing to look at the Quran as a primary source," I wanted to get to the reason for the evening. "I have to tell you there's nothing simple or direct about the text at all levels."

"What do you mean 'at all levels'?"

I explained, "There's the level that one understands from a ba-sic reading of the text. And then there are the levels underneath that have hidden meaning, some say as many as seven levels."

"How can you know where you are in your understanding? How does this affect certainty of belief or knowledge?"

Alsop amplified my pain, and I wanted this part of the evening to conclude. "I would like to say it's possible to know." But I couldn't say it.

We finished dessert and coffee, John left for his home, and Alsop and I went up to his hotel room.

"John told me a little about your concerns, about going to sleep easily and also about your falling spells."

"Do you have any idea what it could be? All along I've thought it was just my peculiarity."

"I have some thoughts about what it is, but I need some more information. Tell me about your going to sleep so easily. When did it begin?'

"I think when I was in grammar school. My teachers noted it but I had no trouble learning what I needed to, so they let it go."

"Anybody else in your family have the same thing?"

"My father has always gone to sleep at odd times. And his father, he was a pearl diver, they used to joke about how he would fall out of the dhow when he went to sleep during the voyage."

"And then there are these falling spells. What's the story on them?"

"They're really embarrassing. They happen when I have no expectation of them, when there's a loud noise that surprises me, or sometimes when I'm overcome with emotion. My body completely loses the strength to remain standing and I fall. It happens at the most difficult times, and people think there's something wrong with me."

"Do you remain awake?"

"I'm perfectly awake during them."

"Are there any other parts to it?"

"I'm not sure what you mean."

"Well, do you experience anything unusual in the early morning before you rise?"

"It's hard for me to say what's unusual—perhaps everyone has this. Sometimes I wake up and can't move. It seems like a long time, but it's probably pretty brief. It used to frighten me a lot, now less so."

"I can tell you what you have—you have all the components— first there's going to sleep easily and inconveniently, and the falls, they're called cataplexy, and finally the sleep paralysis. We call the condition narcolepsy."

"Is it a disease?"

'You'd have to tell me that. It won't kill you, unless you have an auto accident on account of it."

And it could kill someone else.

"It shouldn't get worse."

"Is there any treatment?"

"Yes, there are medicines that may help."

"Does the medicine make it go away?"

"It would help."

"Would it alter the sleep paralysis in the morning?"

"Very likely."

How would I feel about losing the early morning events and the white camel? I'd come to feel that the camel was my only genuine source of knowing, something that originated outside me. "There's something else I should tell about the early morn- ing paralysis. I feel I'm awake, but I have dreams. They're quite real."

"They're not dreams in the usual sense. They're called hypno- gogic hallucinations."

"Am I insane then?"

"No, you're quite sane."

"And the medicine could make the hallucinations disappear?"

"I can't tell you for sure, but it's likely. Do you want me to get the medicine for you?"

I had long considered the possibility the white camel would terminate his visits, and I prayed he would not do so. I would not sacrifice the end of this relationship voluntarily. "No, I appreciate your thoughts and the diagnosis. I don't want medicine." I was firmly in the camel's clutches.

CHAPTER 27

All the Riches of Kuwait
are Mine

The years from 1972 to 1982 were a period of economic, emotional, and social distress brought on by my desire to alter my personal condition. I was impelled by the need to know the truth of Islam, at the same time frustrated by the impossibility of the task, desirous of preserving our status in the community, and urged on by my love for Rabea, which remained the only focus of my life that lacked duality. The white camel intervened at times, not always helpfully but always enigmatically, enough so to be a source of confusion, confusion I didn't need, but relished nevertheless.

These issues revolved around Rabea. The difficulty for her in the Al-Tamimi household had increased to the point that I was distressed for her well-being in the contentious atmosphere. My mother, Fatima, had concluded for reasons unclear to me that Rabea was an inadequate wife. Her childlessness only added to the problem. The wives of Suhayb were at best unpleasant and usually condescending. Rabea remained cheerful, never entering into conflict. So it was from this situation I felt compelled to extract Rabea. But I couldn't achieve this without greater economic independence, enough to secure a separate household.

Rabea, then, was my excuse for entering the Kuwaiti race for riches. Perhaps by this means, I would be able to rescue her. Kuwait, as a small Gulf State in the first stages of remarkable economic development, seemed the ideal environment to achieve the wealth needed to strike out from the family. My objective was to remove Rabea from the family turmoil. In reality the aim was to remove myself.

In December 1969 Saudi Arabia and Kuwait had agreed upon their borders, particularly as they related to known oil reserves, and the so-called neutral zone matter became a non-issue. Thus, the cooperation of the two states was assured in the border area. While it required several years for the process to be consolidated into a productive financial plan of management, this was accomplished and the oil was pumped from the sand in great and valuable quantities. The accumulation of vast wealth was set in motion, and by 1972 the results were boundless by any prior measure. Both States had agreed to share equally in the petroleum production in the area both on and offshore.

Further economic success had been set in motion by the Arab-Israeli conflicts. Thanks to the 1967 oil embargo, which had minimal effect, but which defined the pattern, and the 1973 embargo, which had considerable effect, world dependence on Arab oil increased dramatically, and the money flowed into the Kingdom of Saudi Arabia and the little State of Kuwait.

I saw I could make the best of this scenario, but to do this independently of Suhayb would require cunning. Suhayb was firmly entrenched as the executive of the family businesses, which had long since expanded from the farming enterprise to include an international trading company, retail businesses, and a clever connection to the burgeoning oil industry.

The key to my success in gaining a significant portion of the family money lay in the physical setup and transformation occurring near Ahmadi, the little community just south of Kuwait City. Ahmadi was in the heart of the new oil fields. The British government had redirected British expatriate engineers from India to the little oil town. Ahmadi quickly took on the characteristics of a British outpost colony with tree-lined streets and modest-sized, attractive, single-level houses in the Western ranch style. The training of Kuwait engineers began in earnest, and simultaneously Kuwait's holding interest in the oil revenues gradually increased through the cooperation of the two partners, Gulf Oil (Chevron) and British Petroleum. Oil tankers were now loaded at the Sea Island Terminal, which was ten miles offshore of Mina Al-Ahmadi. By the end of 1975, to my delight, the ownership of the foreign oil companies had been fully transferred to Kuwait. Ahmadi boomed, and it was far enough from the rest of family to allow us respite.

It was into this complex and productive system I inserted myself and, by default, Rabea. I proposed to Suhayb that I take on the management of the family's oil operations with the reasoning that this could best be accomplished with me on site in Ahmadi. This seemed reasonable to Suhayb as he was fully engaged in the trading business in the city and also in his role as imam. The immediate result of this agreement was that we relocated to Ahmadi, taking up residence in one of the British style bungalows.

* * *

Rabea was ecstatic. For the first time in her life, she was free to form her own household. She didn't want to bring any of the family servants, but I insisted on the basis that not to do so would detract from our status. To Rabea's further joy, Divina was asked to return from the Phillippines.

Rabea found herself in the midst of an English-speaking neighborhood and for the first time she was able to expand her language skills from reading, which she had taught herself, to the spoken form. And like everything else she attempted, she succeeded. Rabea quickly formed several female friendships in the neighborhood, most closely with Lydia Mortimer, who lived next door with her engineer husband. The two women set about to teach each other their respective languages.

As the language sessions progressed, Rabea learned that Lydia was a Christian who went to the city on the weekends to attend the NECK. Rabea cautiously broached the topic, and Lydia was shocked to learn the young Arab woman with typical dress and head covering was indeed a Christian. "I didn't know any Kuwaitis were Christian."

"I don't know any others. There must be others, but I don't know them. I've never told anyone but my husband. You mustn't tell anyone, please."

The two women became inseparable and soon I became acquainted with Lydia's husband, Albert, who was able to advise me in the oil business ventures.

* * *

With the increase in flow of funds into the tiny country, the opportunity for greed grew exponentially and with it came political turmoil within the government. My ties with such a large number of different groups, including the regular diwaniya, the Emir's Sharia committee, and now the new group of Brits in Ahmadi, placed me in the strategic position. And as Suhayb had loosened his control over the family's oil interests, I set about making the best of it for Rabea and me.

My job description, as assigned by Suhayb, was the management of the family's major equipment company, Al-Tamimi Oil Supply. I set up the billing and collection component on site. As a side project, and totally unknown to Suhayb, I arranged for some of the work to be split off into the sale of tools and electrical equipment related to the oil business, the Kuwait Tool and Electric. The assets of the two companies were comingled, but the income was separate. I considered that the arrangement was not

entirely ethical in terms of normal business practices, but I justi-
fied the existence of the second company based on the need to
obscure some of the income from the government regulators. In
reality I hid the fact I was using the funds of Al-Tamimi Oil Supply to purchase goods for my own Kuwait Tool and Electric.

With the rapidly increasing oil income and the complexity
of the operation, the government had become fearful that funds
were being diverted from the Emir's coffers. The arrangement in
operation was that 60 percent of the oil income was to go to the
Kuwait government and 40 percent divided between Gulf Oil and
British Petroleum. While there were certainly Kuwaitis who were
diverting the government's funds to their own accounts, this was
not the case with my operation. My fear, however, was that the
government regulators would discover my family indiscretion.

My life had become a balancing act in just about every respect:
the physical separation of Rabea and me from the rest of my family, my continuing religious duplicity, which required concealment if I was to function in Kuwaiti society, my work with the
committee, which required me to impede their progress, the
challenge of operating two simultaneous businesses, one in secret, and my work at the university, which required me to teach
Islamic history and law as if I had full confidence in it. Rabea was
the one steady point of reference.

From the Kuwait Tool and Electric Company, I amassed considerable funds. I maintained the Al-Tamimi Oil Supply books in
the office. While there were two assistants in the office, I made it
clear to them that the handling of the finances was my job only.
I kept the books of the Tool and Electric Company separate and
brought them home each day from the office in Ahmadi. I locked
up the ledger each night.

Rabea questioned my secrecy about the finances in Ahmadi.
"Yacoub, perhaps I can help you with the books. You seem so
concerned about them."

"Never mind. I can take care of it."

"But I want to help you."

"I said never mind."

Rabea withdrew from the challenge and let the matter go for the time.

My anxiety built as the time for the yearly governmental audit approached. I hurried into Khaldiya campus on the days I was to teach, and then back to Ahmadi to pour over the ledgers of the two businesses. Rabea's questions again arose, "Why are you so concerned? Is something wrong?"

"The government auditors will look at the business books."

"Why the concern?" She persisted as if she must know of the fraud.

As the auditors descended upon Ahmadi, anxiety was elevated in the local community. The knowledge was widespread that finances of the operation throughout the community were not clean.

Two auditors were assigned to each of the ten private Kuwaiti contractors in Ahmadi. Of the two assigned to me, one was Bassem Al-Kusai and the second, Abdullah Al-Fatah, a member of the Sharia committee. Abdullah was of a conservative bent with long beard and short dishdasha. I was partially relieved but still concerned as Abdullah brought the Al-Ghabani episodes back to mind.

Bassem and Abdullah were respectful of my family's status. "Where shall we begin?" was their opening ploy. At the same time, rumors were spreading of indictments in the Ahmadi community. The Emir did not intend to tread lightly with the matter of the income. I knew I had not taken any of the State's oil income money, but I was worried the untidy accounts would become evident and eventually reported to Suhayb, who would rightfully be furious.

Bassem set about reviewing the books of Al-Tamimi Oil Supply. I directed Abdullah to the Tool and Electric books, thinking as long as he could keep the review separate, the misuse of funds would not be detected.

Abdullah, however, saw that the amount of funds used to purchase goods for Tool and Electric was too high to be explained by the assets and income of the company. He cornered me. "Yacoub, I am concerned about the Tool and Electric books."

"Yes, what's your concern?"

"How were you able to purchase all the equipment for sale? This is not a matter that concerns the purpose of our audit. I just want to know."

"I am trying to achieve a balance between the businesses."

"But there is the appearance of funds transfer that some might consider inappropriate." I knew he was referring to Suhayb. "Don't worry. I won't reveal this. But you must know you may have the opportunity in our committee of swaying your views to my way of thinking about Sharia law and its implementation."

"I understand your point completely." Once again I was faced with the same practical and rational dilemma, practical because I must maintain my posture in the community and rational because I could not land on solid ground in my personal views of Islam.

CHAPTER 28

Back to Sharia

For the next meeting of the committee we were to take up the potentially poisonous topic of criminal law. I knew this was where Abdullah was aiming. The areas of family, civil, and personal Sharia law were laced with enough difficulties, but the criminal aspects were mainly what separated Kuwait from the Saudis.

I concentrated on the example of Sharia law where the punishment of theft was amputation of the hands. For this punishment to be carried out, the thief must take private property. The thief must not have vital need of the property. The property must have value, and there must be witnesses. I recalled that all of these fit Suhayb's childhood attempt to cut off my hand.

Abdullah led off this discussion by stating how eminently wise and fair the principles were. Many in the committee meeting were surprised when I nodded in agreement.

"The reasoning behind the components Abdullah has enunciated is quite logical. First, there are many forms of ownership. The first criterion refers to the possibility of community property, which does not count for amputation. Second, the thief may be forgiven in part if he needs the property for survival. Third, obviously the property must have some definite value and not be trivial. Finally, there must be credible witnesses. The law here demonstrates the wisdom and clarity of thinking of Sharia and Islam itself."

Abdullah smiled slightly in acknowledgement of his momentary victory. His glance toward me indicated the debt over our business arrangement had been paid, at least in part.

But as an academician I was able to parse a subject into pieces sufficiently small to render any outcome unclear. "I definitely agree with Abdullah in regard to the logic of this law. If it is administered to all equally, then clearly it is fair." Abdullah remained satisfied. But I continued, "We must also listen to the wisdom of the community. Remember Mohammed said 'my community will never agree upon error.'" I reminded the committee that the *ijma*, or the consensus of the wise community, is the third source of Sharia law, after the Quran and the Sunnah (the normal practices of Islam). "The *ijma* is the conclusion of our community, and whether we agree or not here tonight, this means the entire community in conjunction with the expert religious authorities must reach a consensus."

I managed to agree with Abdullah but at the same time lay the groundwork to dispose of the criminal aspects of Sharia law.

The question arose, "So what is our conclusion about Sharia amputation? Our professor tells us that it is fair and logical. But what if the voice of the community says 'no'?"

"What are we to report to the Emir on this matter?"

"Let us report where our discussion stands at present."

I was alarmed they were even having this discussion about amputation as a possibility. I could answer others about Islam but never to my own satisfaction. I departed feeling I had achieved the necessary result with Abdullah but not in my own mind. As I drove out to Ahmadi, I was awakened by the horn of the driver behind me at a traffic light.

CHAPTER 29

Rabea and Lydia

Rabea felt Lydia was her pillar. Now she was able to relate in a normal way to another Christian on a regular basis, and the arrival of Divina back from the Philippines added to this mix. Lydia invited Rabea to the church in the city, but of course she could not go, so much of Rabea's information about what it meant to be a Christian came from Lydia and Divina. The three met several times a week and discussed their lives and their families.

Rabea finally became pregnant, and she shared her elation with Lydia. The baby was expected in the fall of 1974.

Later I pieced together what Rabea had shared with the women. The focus of Rabea's thoughts centered on my double-dealing suffering. But Rabea loved me and didn't dwell on my pain.

I was due home late from diwaniya, but I did not arrive. When Rabea awoke at 3 AM to find our bed was empty, she rose and went next door to Lydia, who could only comfort her. They had no way to reach me.

At 8 AM Suhayb phoned and informed Rabea I had been in an auto accident and was in Mubarak Hospital in the Jabriya section of the city.

* * *

I was aware of Rabea's presence, but I couldn't move, nor respond. It was as if the brief morning episodes of paralysis had settled into a never-ending dream. The dream lasted so long that I began to relish the experience, but this didn't last.

The sand was swirling around me. The experience was tactile, auditory, and visual. I could feel the sand particles stinging my skin. I recalled the day on the Gulf Road in a sand storm with my mother wrapping an ice cream cone in a napkin so it would remain clean. The sound of the wind in the sand produced a high-pitched whine. My vision was partially obscured but I could see forms. Out of the sand, slowly the form of the white camel appeared. And the experience began to diminish in pleasantness. Why did his appearance, his character, trouble me? The white camel was puzzled by the intensity of the storm. He seemed to wander about, unsure of his objective. This was unlike his usual, confident demeanor. Then, it became clear the camel was in pain. He writhed like a woman giving birth. But the writhing was unproductive. After a time, what seemed like a long time, the animal stopped, and the storm ceased. Then, it was over.

* * *

I did not regain consciousness for two days. Rabea was there when I awakened, and she was complaining of abdominal pain. At three months of pregnancy she knew this was not normal, and soon, the baby was lost. Lydia was there for her as she was taken down to the hospital's emergency area. Had the white camel delivered this dream message to me?

* * *

It was another two days before I recovered sufficiently to return home, and I had failed to deliver real support to Rabea over the loss of the baby. The only favorable component was that, since I was confined at home for two weeks, Rabea and I now had the opportunity to talk without interruption.

"It's good to have you here without your having to go off most of the day. I'm sorry for all that's happened but thankful for the time."

"Who do you thank?"

"That's an odd question. The answer should be the same for us both. I thank God, of course."

"Rabea, you're so straightforward in everything you do and say."

"You mean I'm simple."

"No, you're definitely not simple. In many ways, you're a puzzle to me."

"I'm your wife. I see you struggle with that silly committee, that's one thing, but my immediate concern is what you're doing with the business and that you're hiding something from Suhayb. I don't know anything about business, but I feel what you're doing isn't right, or else you wouldn't try to conceal it."

"I'm doing it for us, so we can separate ourselves from the family."

"I don't accept that. We've already separated ourselves from the family. I won't press further. There's more to it than that. The whole thing goes deeper. I've seen you depress yourself over the committee, of course, but anything that has to do with Islam sets you off. You dream. I've heard you speak about the white camel. Why don't you turn away from giving meaning to these dreams? I don't know your camel, but what you say about him frightens me."

"It's not that easy. The dreams don't go away. They're part of me. I don't want them to recede."

"Yacoub, what do you want?"

'I don't know if I can say this clearly. I should be able to articulate what I want. When I first studied Islam, I saw it as a definite, clear entity. As God revealed it, it should be possible to know the truth with absolute certainly. That's what I wanted. But that gets further and further away instead of nearer."

"I'm sorry."

"I envy you. You read one book, and you believe it. Of course you don't really know for certain if it's true, you couldn't, but I know you believe it completely. I can see that. How does that happen?"

"There's a verse in one of Paul's letters, just a part of a verse. It says 'with the heart one believes.' That's what happened to me."

"I don't know if I can continue."

"I'll try to help you. I love you."

CHAPTER 30

There's Enough for All

I said to Rabea, "There seems to be no end to it, this boundless wealth coming from the ground." Few Kuwaitis escaped its benefits. But some families, notably the Al-Tamimi, reaped benefits beyond any imagining of it. Most of this remarkable success was attributable to Suhayb's management skills and his charismatic personality. I had never thought my brother to be particularly clever, but when it came to making money and important friends, he didn't have an equal in Kuwait.

The 1973 oil embargo directed against Western countries raised oil prices, but in reality the increase was superfluous, as the world was too addicted to the fluid. The Kuwaiti government fully grasped the range of possibilities and began using the oil money for a variety of investments that would serve the little State for years into the future and beyond. In 1975 the Kuwaiti government took over full control of the Kuwait Oil Company, thus directing proceeds into the Emir's coffers.

Suhayb had placed himself in such proximity to the Sabahs that the change in ownership did not perturb him. The Al-Tamimi Oil Supply Company flourished to an even greater degree. I worried Suhayb might discover my questionable management of the Kuwait Tool and Electric Company, but after a while I recognized Suhayb had known all along and merely tolerated the siphoning off of funds from one company to the other. Such methods were commonplace in Kuwaiti business, and there was enough money for all. This family example of questionable business practice was unexceptional in Kuwait and simply not worth Suhayb's time or concern. Suhayb's laissez faire attitude made the unethical practice seem acceptable and therefore forgettable to me. To Rabea's continuing concern, I continued the practice, but I no longer harbored guilt over it.

But such doings did not always lead to good will, and certainly it was worse when more than one immediate family was involved. The increased availability of wealth led to greater strife and competition, and Kuwait became a hotbed of rumor, unproductive diversity of opinion, and infighting among groups. If the question were posed as to what was responsible for the underlying social turmoil, a variety of answers might be given. I listed them mentally: religious differences, conflicts over the Lebanese civil war, the invasion of Kuwait by a growing ex-patriot community, particularly the large Palestinian faction, and concern over relations with Iran and Iraq, but the underlying wealth was the real unsettling component that had been introduced too rapidly into the society.

In August of 1976, Emir Sabah Al-Salim al-Sabah saw the fabric of the State torn by the presence of the strife manifest on a daily basis in the newspapers and in the forum of the national assembly. He therefore dissolved the parliament. The immediate reason was over a dispute between Crown Prince Jaber and the Parliament. The assembly was not reconvened until 1981. All this diminished the popularity of the Sabahs at a critical time, but the wealth of the country remained both a detriment and a savior.

These ongoing events helped obscure my personal strife, which continued to be internal and accentuated by self-doubts and natural double-mindedness. As the money accumulated, my family's living conditions elevated beyond anything I had anticipated. Still, I distrusted my own abilities and direction, and Rabea simply did not care about the wealth. The gold she had stolen from her family remained under our bed, no longer a source of concern for her. So the wealth was of no advantage, other than to extract us from the family compound.

Into this social maelstrom Sheik Jaber became Emir in 1977 after the death of Sabah. This mattered a great deal to the Al-Tamimi household. But once again it was Suhayb who had ingrained himself into the proper setting. He frequented Jaber's palace and was even there at times when no photographs were taken for the evening news.

Rumors traveled the country in forty-eight-hour cycles, and I was impressed Suhyab was wise enough not to be the subject of them. He did not inform us about his interactions with the Emir. Moreover, I didn't want to know. Most of these situations were more intrigue and deceit at some level and therefore information about them would only add to my insecurity.

In February 1981 Jaber allowed the assembly election to go forward. To the surprise of virtually everyone, Suhayb did not offer himself for election. Given his name and popularity in the male community of Kuwait, he would have been elected easily.

Then, the ministerial staff of the State was announced, and Suhayb was named Minister of Finance. I had expected Suhayb would take some position in the government, but this was unanticipated. Suhayb was respected for his personal leadership characteristics and his faithfulness as a devout Muslim, but he had no formal knowledge of economics and finance. His main statement as he was introduced as Finance Minister was that he intended to promote the Islamic principle of no interest on loans. Of course everyone present nodded in agreement, but all knew that the cost of loaning to another was not zero and that the only real business of business was profit by one at the expense of another. They smiled in concern over their new Minister of Finance.

The Kuwait Finance House had been established in 1977 as the first Islamic bank in Kuwait. Since its inception, Suhayb had been on its board of directors. He stated his intent to remain on the board, and while some considered that his position as Minister of Finance might represent a potential conflict of interest, the matter was put aside. Suhayb proceeded with the duties of both positions. No one could handle the monumental job of regulating the exponentially expanding Kuwait economy. Suhayb said he was aware of the burgeoning problems and consoled me, stating that, if only Islamic principles were followed, the economy could be controlled and maintained.

But Islamic banking principles were not in play in the big picture. The Kuwait Finance House was the only institution that kept the principles in operation. The main ideas, that usury was abhorrent and that risk should be shared for the good of the whole, were not concepts that had ignited the economy in the first place. The fire of the economy was the obvious availability of the riches of Kuwait and the innate desire of many to possess it and profit from it.

The problem was fueled by an earlier event. In 1977, with the occurrence of a minor stock market crash, the then-Finance Minister had rescued the investors, who had suffered seriously. Along with everyone else, I adopted the illusion that the government had sufficient wealth and the will to save the unwise or unlucky investor. Consequently, confidence in the market exceeded real value.

The regular, lawfully regulated Kuwait stock market was too small to absorb the funds that were waiting to be invested. In addition, major families who traded large blocks of stocks dominated trading. Although the Al-Taminis were indeed wealthy, we did not approach the level of the super rich.

As a consequence of these coexisting events, and despite Suhayb's intent to preserve honor and Islamic principles, the Souk al-Manakh developed. I wondered about the wisdom of the idea.

Perhaps the Manakh was the shrewd Arab trader gone out of control. But Suhayb was not open to critical thoughts, and he allowed the phenomenon to commence.

The Souk al-Manakh began in a hall previously used for camel trading. At the time I wondered if the lingering smell from the previous venture should have served as a warning.

Ironically the Manakh ostensibly operated in the broad tradition of Arab honor, relying on all investors to keep their word as their bond. This was manifest in the peculiar Kuwaiti custom at the time of issuing postdated checks as the way to pay for the stock purchased. As the stocks all rose dramatically in value, this procedure was deemed safe, because there would always be funds to pay the check when the date came due.

Westerners were encouraged to join in the windfall. Few did. The stocks rose to lofty heights. As the Kuwaiti investors said repeatedly, "You in the US don't understand what's happening here. There's never been anything like this in the world economy. The wealth we have knows no boundaries. It can't fail."

Even Suhayb was swept into it. His own use of postdated checks gave license and approval to the process. The accumulation of funds on paper in the Al-Tamimi accounts was astronomical. To his credit, he placed the funds in the Kuwait Finance House with the encouragement that they be used in an interest-free economy, and this act accomplished much for the welfare of those who needed funds for homes, manufacturing equipment, and reliable outside investments. This was well reported by the newspapers, as was his design, increasing Suhayb's popularity.

I saw the wealth amassed by Souk al-Manakh participants. It would not be fair to Rabea not to participate. I joined the excitement against Rabea's protestations.

But there was another reason I joined the financial experiment. I continued to receive letters from Arizona. Previously these had contained only a photograph of a darkly handsome and growing young man. There was never a return address. I placed these carefully in the drawer of my desk at the university. They were a silent reminder of past indiscretions, compounding my guilt. Then, a letter arrived with a return address on the outside and inside, in addition to the usual photo, was a letter from Sattie:

Dear Yacoub,

I am sure this letter finds you well. I have read about the success of your family in Kuwait and heard well of your performance at the university. I have colleagues in the region who are complimentary of your scholarship.

I would not bother you for anything were it not of such weight that you would want to know. My husband of many years has divorced me. He has refused to pay for our son's education. Perhaps you can guess why.

Your son is exceptional. He will go far in his studies. But after the divorce I do not have sufficient funds to support his education in the necessary manner. I ask not for me but for him.

As ever,
Sattie

P.S. We are having a three-day conference on Islamic affairs in March. It would be good if you could come and give a lecture on Sharia. Let me know . . .

I set about participating in the Manakh and told myself it was for the right reasons. I put aside the invitation.

Rabea kept her concerns to herself for a time, but she couldn't restrain herself and see me participate in the debacle. "Yacoub, I'm worried about your investments in the Manakh. It doesn't make sense."

"Rabea, you're a good wife. Let that be your job."

"I think this is part of my being a good wife. Anything that is purchased must have value. I don't see the value. Lydia told me her husband saw one of the companies you've bought stock in when he was in Manama—the Gulf Purchasing Venture.'

"I think it's a very strong company—the stock has tripled."

"Then sell it now. Lydia said the company was just a sign on a dilapidated building. No one was there. There were no employees."

"But we're making so much money."

"We don't need more money. We have everything. Now, we really have everything. I'm pregnant again."

I embraced Rabea. Perhaps we did have everything.

That night I slept hard and nearly without turning. Then, in the early morning, the white camel came again. He had not visited for some time. The white camel appeared content as he wandered among stocks of lush vegetation and abundant clear water. Then, the camel saw the perfect she-camel, and he wandered after her leaving the wealth of food and water behind. The white camel vanished with the she-camel.

The next morning I sold my Manakh holdings for the best cash price I could get, cashed whatever postdated checks were available and due, and paid the postdated checks I had signed.

The Manakh had the third-largest market capitalization in the world behind the US and Japan. The total amount was a ridiculous $100 billion, which arguably was more than the total value of all Kuwaiti hard assets. The final dagger occurred when eight investors who called themselves the "Cavaliers" issued a total of $55 billion in postdated checks. A passport office employee, Jassim al-Mutawa, was responsible for $14 billion by himself. Needless to say, his account was eventually listed as "overdrawn." All told, 29,000 postdated checks adding up to $93 billion were written on the shares of companies that were each practically worthless. As the checks could not be paid, the Manakh collapsed in August 1982.

Rabea and the white camel saved our household. Suhayb was not saved, and his losses and the Al-Tamimi family losses were considerable. But the losses were survivable. The Manakh disaster had happened on Suhayb's watch as Finance Minister, and therefore his post as a minister could not be salvaged. As a matter of honor he was compelled to resign. Jaber accepted his resignation reluctantly, but he accepted it nevertheless.

But Suhayb somehow preserved his standing in the community. My status followed Suhayb's. The newspaper published the fact that much of his wealth earned through the Manakh had been deposited in the Kuwait Finance House where it was used properly according to Sharia practices. His postdated checks, which were of no value, were written on other banks.

CHAPTER 31

Were the Lessons Learned?

As 1982 closed out, the Iran–Iraq war, begun in 1980, had had little direct influence, but its growing significance in the region, along with the tactics used by both combatants, began to take center stage in regional politics. Little Kuwait, tucked between the two floundering giants, had the greatest vulnerability both in terms of financial assets that were at risk and also from potential spillover of the conflict itself. As an observer of these events, my concern rose over the safety of my family.

At first, and unpredictably, there were border incursions from Iraqi forces coming down into Kuwait as far as Al-Rawdatain north of Kuwait City and also to the west over the desert. These were not serious attacks from a military standpoint, for if they had been so, there would have been no adequate defense. Rather it was clear Saddam Hussein was sending a message to the Kuwait government that their borders were indeed vulnerable and that they were at significant risk. As a defense, the only refuge of little Kuwait was to make a political choice and back one of the two giants to the north. The Kuwait government chose the Arabs over the Persians.

Despite his failure in managing the Manakh stock exchange and his necessary departure from the Finance Ministry, Suhayb still had the respect of the community. His position continued to be favorable, based on his family name and his respectability in the religious sector. He remained a frequent visitor at the Emir's palace. Although he had never joined the Kuwait military, Suhayb developed acquaintances with a number of generals and enjoyed promising relationships among them.

I was ever adrift, even after my financial success in the Manakh following my timely withdrawal from the market. There were considerations not resolved: my son in Arizona whom I did not know, my strained situation with my family, and most troubling, my growing uncertainty about Islam itself.

Why does it matter? I have everything I need here. I should be content. Rabea will soon have a child. We were wealthy by any standard. But what had been the quest of my early and still young life was the need to resolve Islam as a revealed truth. And then there were the recurring visitations of the white camel. The juxtaposition of the camel on one side and Islam on the other made me question whether one or both were deceiving me. A man in his forties should put aside such worries and deal with the present, but the present was ever before me in the form of morning visitations and obsessive thoughts.

I accepted Sattie's invitation. I would go to Tucson in March 1983 for the conference. I told Rabea about the trip, not thinking that the baby was due the first of April. *A husband's folly.* Rabea's facial response to the news of the trip surprised me. I thought she would be proud of my international recognition.

"If the baby comes, I will be left only with my own family, what's left of them, and yours in the city. It will be terrible."

"But I've already accepted the invitation and the program is set." How I wanted to go! I wasn't sure if was because of my son or Sattie. "Lydia and Divina will be here. They will help."

"But the family won't understand."

"I'm sorry. I really must go."

The topics of the conference were assigned. I was to speak on Sunni interpretation of Sharia law. The Iraqi scholar Ahmad Ibn Yusuf was to speak on the Shia interpretation.

The winter of 1982–83 was comprised of a mixture of tasks: teaching at the university which required minimal preparation, consolidation of my financial obligations and resources, which were now strong, a holding action with the Sharia committee, wherein my objective was to limit progress, preparation for the conference in Arizona, which did not require much thought, and finally the attention Rabea required in her second pregnancy knowing she had lost the first.

Rabea's morning sickness abated in the winter, and the pregnancy progressed well. I took her to the obstetrician at Maternity Hospital near the Sabah hospital complex. By the time I was to leave for the US, the doctor was encouraging that the pregnancy would reach term and that her delivery would likely await my return. I consoled myself, and to some degree Rabea, and I departed.

I arrived at the Tucson Sheraton and slept for twelve hours. I was awakened by a call from the lobby. It was Sattie.

"Yacoub, I'm sorry to awaken you from your trip, but we must get organized for the conference. Can you come down? I'll wait for you in the lounge."

I showered quickly, mustered strength for whatever awaited, dressed in a yellow polo shirt and cream slacks and got on the elevator. I was anxious and sweating, partly from the hot shower.

I went to the lounge and saw Sattie in a corner with a tall drink. Not surprisingly, she looked nearly twenty years older. She was heavier but otherwise well kept. She wore blue pants and a blouse carelessly buttoned; the habit had not changed.

I was thankful she didn't rise to greet me, as I was unsure whether I should kiss her on the cheek, embrace her gently, or merely shake hands. She extended her hand from her sitting position and made the decision for me.

"Yacoub, for many reasons I'm glad you came. I wasn't sure you would. I wouldn't have blamed you if you had declined." I didn't know how to respond. "Of course, we needed you for the conference. You're now one of the leading academics in Sharia law, even though you've sequestered yourself in little Kuwait. And I want to talk about our son. And then, I just wanted to see you again. I know I was rough with you before. I know that and I won't be again."

I was not sure of the direction of the conversation or even why she had come to the hotel to meet him. "Where shall we start? How is our son?"

"He's brilliant and introspective like you. You've seen his picture, how much he looks like you."

"I want to see him, meet him."

"No, definitely not. He'd know in a moment." Once again, Sattie proclaimed her control. "He's been accepted at Stanford. I can't pay for it, and my husband, former husband, won't."

"Of course I will. I'll write a check for $20,000. That should get him started for a year or two."

Was the money Sattie's reason for the meeting? She informed me the conference participants would meet at her home the next evening.

I arrived at the assigned time, but there were no other guests. Sattie opened the door, smiled and invited me in. She was dressed in blue slacks and a loose blouse. Her hair was down. I couldn't escape. Sattie still possessed the authority as my professor. I left two hours later ashamed of my lack of resistance and all the more guilty for what I had done to betray Rabea.

The next day I met my Sharia counterpart, Ahmad Ibn Yusuf. Ahmad was a stunted little man, self-assured, and really quite unpleasant with bad breath. He didn't let me forget he was from a great country and that Kuwait was a minor player in the momentous regional conflict. His first entry was to recall in florid detail the history of the caliphate in Iraq and the great tragedy in Karbala where Hussein, the son of Ali, was martyred. He inquired, as a Shia to a Sunni, "Where is your source of authority? You consult with whomever seems good at the time."

I offered the answers expected with an outline of my talk that was to be delivered, which consisted of the usual Sunni sources of Sharia. I didn't argue, as there was no reason to try and dispatch the unpleasant little man. Also, I didn't share the same depth of conviction, and victory was of little interest to me. I had already failed morally. What was the point?

The conference from then on was painful and boring. I had heard everything many times, and the material was directed at the level of the senior college and graduate student in Islamic studies. Sattie hardly spoke to me. She had gotten what she wanted. My only departing words to her were: "Let me know if you need more funds, and I'll send them to you." She nodded agreement. Now I really had no choice.

But the idea of the authority, as it existed in Shia but not in Sunni Islam, gave me pause. On the endless plane ride back to Kuwait, first the stop at Kennedy and then at Heathrow, I couldn't sleep. Moral and theological failure haunted me. And now the sad idea of a different, perhaps more reliable source of authority kept coming back to me. I resolved to give this continuing consideration, quietly, for I could not reveal it to his colleagues in Kuwait. Had it not been for repeated lapses of moral and ethical practice, the matter would not have been so consuming, but I needed a workable alternative.

I arrived in Ahmadi to be welcomed by the onset of Rabea's labor. Rabea had already called her relatives who remained in Kuwait, and her uncle was on his way to Ahmadi. With all the awkwardness involved between the two families because of the events leading to the reasons for the arranged marriage, I stepped into my role quickly and raced Rabea to the hospital. I was sleepy and stiff from the long flight, feeling guilty for the indiscretion, but I was able to muster sufficient strength to act properly concerned, which I was indeed.

The trip to Maternity Hospital was an hour from Ahmadi, and Rabea was straining with each contraction. We arrived at the door on the seaside of the hospital and the attendants took Rabea away. The sun was glinting off the waters of the Gulf in a light breeze. Rabea was crying. I went to the main lobby and tried to get someone to tell me what to do. Rabea's uncle arrived about the same time, and we spoke superficially. Six hours passed, and my travel fatigue settled over me like the fog off the Gulf. I was summoned to see Rabea, who was holding our daughter.

Rabea was then transferred to the women's ward, which was a large, open room with the women separated by the curtains from each other and from the center of the ward. The families tried to be quiet to preserve each other's peace and privacy. Rabea rested that night alone and by the next morning I was able to spend time privately with her. Rabea's aunt had been there earlier, but she sensed the awkwardness of the situation and left.

As we were enjoying the full sense of the experience, and I held my daughter, loud cries of pain and fear overcame all other sounds. I heard a young woman's screams, and they were clearly not related to labor. I then saw a thin man with a gray dishdasha and gray beard emerge from a curtained bed across the ward. His dishdasha was covered in blood in the front and he held a dagger. He had yelled, "God is Great" several times. He walked out of the ward purposely and proudly. He did not hurry. The young woman's screams diminished and were replaced by the yelling of the nursing staff as they summoned a doctor.

At that time no information was offered to the onlookers, but soon a gurney was brought into the ward, and the gurney then emerged from the curtained area across the ward bearing a covered object. The sheet over the object was stained with blood, and the outcome was clear.

Four days later I took Rabea and Hibah back to Ahmadi. Rabea had chosen the name, Hibah, which means "gift."

The details of the event on the ward gradually emerged. The young mother from a Bedouin family was only fourteen, and she had been unmarried. The man stained in blood with the dagger was her paternal uncle. He made no attempt to conceal his identity. The police interviewed him and when he explained he had no choice but to defend the honor of his family, they inquired where he could be reached and released him pending any legal action. The police did not appear to have control of the situation, and the family was entirely supportive of his action. The twenty-year-old man who was thought to be the father was not considered at fault because he questioned the young girl's virginity. The Kuwait City newspapers reported the event with widely varying editorial interpretations. One wrote, "The heinous crime openly committed by the girl's relative must be punished to the full extent of the law. This is murder."

At the other end of the scale, another said, "The ways of our people cannot be ignored. We are a people of honor, and honor requires its own payment. The payment has been made." And so it went.

The court system was at a loss as to how to deal with the crime or event. The application of law said that a crime had been committed, but they had no stomach for making a courageous choice in either direction.

I learned how the Emir intended to handle the situation by reading the Kuwait Times several days later. I couldn't believe the result, and I felt the matter was directed at me personally. Rabea read it and said nothing. The Emir announced he recognized the importance of the matter in terms of Sharia law. He would therefore turn the decision over to the Glorious Committee for adjudication. To this point the committee had done nothing but chat and report "progress."

Now the committee was critical in terms of a State issue. To make it worse, Malik called me to inform that I was responsible for writing the committee's position paper and that I was expected to present the paper for discussion at the next meeting. The Emir demanded a formal decision. I was paralyzed until I realized the outcome was a foregone conclusion. There would be substantial bantering and bartering back and forth. Time would pass. And the old Bedouin man would not be charged. I therefore crafted a statement that would conform to the anticipated outcome.

The evening of the committee meeting arrived. I read the statement, and immediately the arguing began. Malik stated flatly that the old man should be tried for murder under standard legal procedure. Karam defended the killer's actions because of the need to preserve the honor of the family. There were views in between, and much changing of views. The heat of the day did not subside, and the evening remained uncomfortably warm. Voices were raised periodically, and the farash was afraid to enter the diwaniya to bring tea. Four hours later the committee agreed to adopt my statement and present it to the Emir.

Two weeks later Rabea screamed and summoned me. She was reading the Kuwait Times. "Yacoub, your writing is quoted about the death of the unmarried mother. How could you say this?"

The quote read, "In the name of Allah, the Merciful, the Compassionate, we decree the following in regard to the killing of the sinful woman who bore a child at Maternity Hospital on April 2, 1983. The young woman was guilty of fornication. The young man who was the stated father was also guilty of fornication. The penalty in such cases is often cited as 100 lashes by flogging. However, the hadiths compiled in *Sahih El-Bukhari* also cite death by stoning as a penalty. By the testimony of the man, the woman was not a virgin. As the woman bore a child and her virginity could no longer be established by any means, we must credit his testimony as true. Therefore, the death penalty for her, while not administered under a prescribed circumstance, must be considered fair. The uncle who killed the woman to assuage the honor of the family should not be prosecuted."

Rabea spoke little to me for several days and cloistered Hibah from me.

The slaying of the young mother was soon forgotten by most, and the killer was not prosecuted. The Emir was thankful to the committee and me for the passing of the incident. The consensus of the community for the death penalty was met, as a prime determinant of Sharia law. I was relieved with the fading of memories so quickly. *Now I am finished with the stain of Sharia*, which in this case was a bloody stain.

CHAPTER 32

Perhaps There is Something Else

Azar Isfahani was red-faced, scholarly, pugnacious man who always wore a coat and tie. His family, originally from Iran, had resided in Kuwait since 1915 and therefore were Kuwaiti citizens even though they maintained active connections with others in Iran. Isfahani drove a large, white Mercedes and lived in a palatial estate along the Gulf. The source of his family's obvious wealth, when questioned, was stated offhandedly as "business interests."

He had received his doctoral degree in Islamic studies from the Faculty of Humanities and Literature at Isfahan University in 1970. For reasons that were unclear to the other faculty he was hired as Associate Professor in the fall of 1983. Other than his degree he had accumulated no other academic credentials in the intervening thirteen years. There was speculation he was hired in order to assuage the Shia population in Kuwait that adequate weight was given to their minority view of Islam. This view was doubted, however, as "balance" had never been the dominant societal aim. More likely, it was related to a large contribution that appeared in the departmental coffers.

I took an immediate liking to the man. On his first day Azar invited me to his office for coffee, made from Nescafe and hot water, which I considered careless. Still, I was glad to meet this gregarious, elfin man. Our conversation was light and seemingly for the purpose of getting acquainted, but Azar had remarkable knowledge about my background and even about how I had married Rabea.

Then, Azar changed the direction of the conversation and told a joke about the Emir, which I considered in bad taste. My expression betrayed discomfort, and Azar smiled and shifted the conversation again. Azar had control of the direction of the relationship, and his awareness of this fact kept recurring in my mind.

"I've talked with Malik about your Glorious Committee."

"I'm afraid there's nothing glorious about it."

"Yes, I know, but my friend Malik tells me your input to the committee has been invaluable in its progress."

"Progress has not been the real objective."

"I know that, too. Malik has also told me of your ambivalence."

"My ambivalence to what?"

"To everything, my friend."

The conversation concluded on that note, but Azar pledged another invitation would be forthcoming. And soon Rabea and I were invited for a meal at the Isfahani household. It was a bit unusual we would receive a husband and wife invitation at such an early point in the relationship, but I was curious how this would proceed. And Rabea might find it interesting to converse with Shia women.

As Rabea was breastfeeding Hibah, it was appropriate she would bring the baby. We proceeded down Gulf Road and turned into the residence after driving through the guarded iron gate. In front of the home, surrounded by several fountains, we were ushered out of the vehicle, which was then parked by an attendant around the side of the main building. As was normal practice Rabea and the infant were shown into a separate area with the women while I joined the men.

There were considerably more guests than I expected. All were Shia. Why had we been included? Many of the men had family backgrounds originating in Iran. I had the general image of Shia as conservative in their dress and behavior, generally of lesser means, and more devout in religion. This stereotype was not met by the experience of the evening. The conversation was loud and urged on by the ready availability of expensive whiskey, in which I did not partake. Azar greeted me enthusiastically but then paid me little mind the remainder of the evening. Finally, a lavish meal with kebab torsh and other Persian dishes was served. As the close of the meal signals the traditional time of departure, I rose to leave. Azar said softly, "Thank you for coming and meeting my friends. I know we have much in common, which we can discuss privately. I admire your work and your thinking a great deal."

My puzzlement persisted in the drive home, and Rabea's joined this concern. "Yacoub, why were we invited? It seemed pointless to me. I have nothing to share with the women."

"I don't know. I suppose we'll find out."

Upon arrival at my office the next morning at the university, another letter and photograph from Tucson greeted me. The letter read:

Dear Yacoub,

I enjoyed your visit a great deal. You know this was on two levels—your expert effort at the meeting and, even more, our time alone. That time brought back wonderful memories, which I had doubted could be restored, but indeed they were.

Our son's expenses are greater than I had anticipated. He will need another $20,000 to continue his studies. I know you will be faithful to this request. You may wire the funds to my account at the Bank of Tucson, which is numbered 427-755. My account number is 727-88957.

Thanks again for your concern about our son. I wonder if it is best to write you at the university or whether I should send the letters and photographs to your home address.

As Ever,

Sattie

I put the letter and photo in my desk along with the others. Of course, I would comply with the request, but she was asking for more than what was needed for his education. And clearly the last sentence of her letter was a veiled threat of blackmail. And there would be more requests.

Two weeks passed. The conflict between Iraq and Iran wore itself out in the Kuwaiti newspapers. The population was uncertain whom they should fear, and the financial markets were unstable. Then Azar came round, "Yacoub, please visit my office when you have time."

Later in the day I found Azar. As he looked up from his grading of papers, I sat down and looked about the office. Azar had in the interim decorated his office with well-appointed relics and numerous framed photographs and awards in calligraphic script. Conspicuously absent were the usual academic papers typical of the offices of university professors. There were three citations from the Emir thanking Azar for his generosity, one for a donation to the Kuwait Society for Disabled Children, one for his family's contributions to the Palestine Liberation Organization, and a third for his donation to the university. It was becoming clearer how he had been appointed Associate Professor without further academic credentials. Then, in the corner of the room, less conspicuous, I saw it—a plaque from the University of Arizona thanking him for his generous donation to the School of Islamic Studies. Azar saw my gaze settle there and commented, "Yes, I know you did your PhD work there. I'm acquainted with your mentor, Dr. Allison." My lips numbed as I saw Azar's demeanor change to a more controlling posture. "She told me much about you and your work. Your thesis was very insightful."

"You read my thesis?"

"No, as you know, no one ever reads those things. But I am aware we have much to discuss in that realm, and I'm really looking forward to it. And your friend on the committee, Malik, informed me of your views. I'm sure our talks will be very profitable."

Why should they be profitable?

"I think you're a man who is on a search. So am I. So we join forces, eh? From talking with those who know you, I believe you endeavor to find the truth, at least in the realm of theology." The last phrase hung like a net, whether to save or snare, I wasn't sure.

"Yes, of course, I would relish such a search. And I was very interested by the composition of the group at your recent get-to-gether. The evening altered my concept of the Shia. I had thought of Shia as very conservative in dress and rather modest in material possessions. The group seemed well off, thanks be to God."

"Yes, indeed, thanks be to God, we are blessed. We can introduce you to many financial concepts. One's finances can be quite important, especially in maintaining family homeostasis." Again, Azar's last phrase hung over me.

"I gather from our discussions and my conversations with your friends that you have been wholly concerned with knowing the truth and that you have been frustrated by Sunni Islam." I didn't respond. "Perhaps our concepts can provide the necessary assurance for you. We have a more reliable method than merely the 'consensus' of the community." He referred to one of the pillars of Sunni theology. "Our source of authority is direct from Mohammed and resides in the last Mahdi, who will appear at the last day. Our imams are inspired by the spirit of Allah and the last Mahdi, and they cannot be led into error." Azar expressed the Twelver view of Shia Islam, with which I was well acquainted.

"Yes, I understand your position."

I excused myself for my next class.

CHAPTER 33

Does the White Camel Interfere?

I slept restlessly by Rabea that night, and the infant awoke crying several times. Rabea attended. Only by morning did I sleep soundly and this time the white camel visited in a normal dream state rather than the more common occurrence of intervention during the sleep paralysis that came after awakening.

This time the camel seemed to wander without direction in the open desert on a cloudless day. Then, a sandstorm arose out of the east, seeming to descend on the desert having crossed the Gulf bearing the dust from Iran. How did I know the source of the dust? Azar's intervention? The camel searched through the same dust and, after a time, found a water hole, a deep well. The camel paused awaiting the man who was necessary to draw the water, and the dream concluded. My concern over the significance of the camel deepened further. Was he for my good, or otherwise?

I awoke unsatisfied by the abbreviated sleep and the ambiguous dream. I pledged as an academician to consider the possibilities which were, in order of consideration: the whole matter of the dream message was a creation of my frustrated mind, or perhaps I had completely misinterpreted the information, or perhaps the dream heralded a good outcome with Azar, or finally, my greatest fear, none were correct.

The consensus of the community, according to Sunni Islam, had not answered the affairs of my heart. Perhaps what Azar had said would be a refuge. I would therefore look to what would transpire with Azar.

* * *

And then there was my interaction with John.

"You've told me about Rabea." He referred to her belief.

"I know you won't reveal that to others. The cost to us would be great."

"I know all that, but you can talk to me."

It came to me that John was a strange man, not proud, yet confident, and uninterested in personal goals, yet satisfied with life. *He's different from me—we're friends, but we don't really understand each other.*

* * *

And then, sooner than anticipated, another significant request arrived from Sattie.

The next week I went to Azar's office.

"I've been expecting you—you're unsettled."

"Well, not really, but I thought we could talk."

"I certainly understand you're concerned. I can see that. Is it material or otherwise?"

"It's a little of both. We can explore."

"Do you want to meet with one of our imams?"

I smiled at Azar, whom I was beginning to enjoy. While I did not promise to follow up on Azar's suggestion, I didn't reject it. I went back to Ahmadi that evening, and after eating dinner silently with Rabea, I got back in my car and drove out into the near desert along Magwa Road where I parked the car. The sun was setting, and the sky and sand were a blurry blend of yellow and red. In the evening light the sand and horizon lost their crisp distinction. I spotted a dhub scurrying for its burrow, and that encounter brought back the recollection of my embarrassing attempt to fetch one in the contest with Suhayb. I had hoped to come out to the open desert in order to see the way with clarity, but the evening was not clear.

My search had taken more than twenty years. More than any of my colleagues in the department at Kuwait University, I was intimately familiar with Sunni theology. I hated to admit the search was a failure, and I envied Rabea for all her calmness and inner satisfaction. She and her happy demeanor were the centerpieces of my thoughts, but there was nothing there I could grasp. There could be no harm in looking at the Shia way. I would let Azar know.

Within the week I sat in the home of Hamid Al-Hamadi. Dressed in a black robe with his head bound by a black scarf, Hamid's height was nearly matched by his breadth. I was struck that Hamid's seeming contentment was promoted only by elevating himself to a higher rank than he appeared to deserve. In fact I had never met a man who displayed such pride for so little reason. Hamid sat cross-legged on the couch leaning forward so that his gray, curly beard fell upon his hands folded over his legs at the location where they crossed. Apparently this was his position of pontification because he began to hold forth.

"Well, Yacoub, I'm elated that you've come to see me. I fully understand your position as an accepted authority in your field of Sunni Islam, and it must have taken a great deal of courage to come here. But the fact you are here with me indicates you're truly a wise man. The authority I possess is not awarded by the community, as you know, but by a long history of transmission of authority from the Prophet himself. I myself have been designated authority through the great imam across the Persian Gulf. What I say, therefore, comes from God, because I have been blessed with the necessary insight and wisdom." The sunlight through the window blinded me for a moment. "I pray this gives you confidence in what I say. I know you understand the truth of this transmission from the Prophet. I know also that it will be difficult, considering your situation, for you to come openly in our direction. At least that will be the case for a while. And in time you will understand you cannot avoid us. I look to that day." His soliloquy continued in the same vein for more than an hour. He required little response or affirmation in order to continue.

Finally I sensed a pause, smiled, thanked Hamid profusely, as he seemed to require, and left for Ahmadi. Hamid guided me to the door satisfied with the success of his speech. He seemed certain I was converted to Shiism.

I drove home with ambiguous thoughts. Hamid disgusted me. The man had only his pride to offer. In keeping with my former image of the Shia, Hamid was of modest means and conservative in his manner of life, with the primary exception being his elevated self-image. I found him in sharp contrast to the men at Azar's home. These men I liked, but I wanted no more of Hamid. I had to be circumspect when I talked again with Azar, for I didn't want to abandon the inquiry just yet. There had to be more to it.

I met briefly with Azar in his office the next day. "What did you think of Hamid?" Azar smiled at my lack of response. Then he said, "No matter. It was just a formality. Some of the men I want you to talk with considered the meeting important. Of course, it's not. I'll receive you at my home Saturday evening at 7."

"I'm happy to come. Should I bring Rabea?"

"No, no—this is men only."

Saturday arrived without my knowing the purpose of the meeting. As I drove through the iron gate, there were the same cars observed on the first visit, mostly Mercedes, of a newer and larger vintage than my own. Upon entering the room, really a large hall, where they were gathered, I knew I was not attending a party or celebration. The furniture was gilded in gold paint and the seat cushions were lined thickly with gold thread. Most of the men were dressed in suits, not in the traditional Kuwaiti dishdasha. In addition to Azar, I was greeted by Zain, who identified himself by body language as the organizer of the get-together. He strutted to the front of the room.

After coffee and tea were served, Zain asked all to remain sitting as he rose. "Gentlemen, thank you for attending tonight. As you all are aware (I was not aware), we have in front of us a marvelous opportunity. All of you are financially successful beyond any previous expectation." I did not feel so endowed. "You have had many financial opportunities in the past. All of these contained an element of uncertainty. But Allah has blessed you. Now we must discuss an endeavor devoid of elements of chance. But the level of commitment required of you is high. The risk is personal rather than financial."

I began to sweat under my dishdasha, and my anxiety level rose. I was enclosed by events. I had not been required to come this far. Or was I? Azar seemed to possess critical information about my past.

Zain continued, "All of us have considerable wealth, but only by placing our resources together will we be able to accomplish our end. Once more I emphasize the money you're asked to commit is not at risk. The financial outcome is secured by the information we possess or will possess."

I recalled similar claims about the Manakh and stated them aloud.

"We are speaking tonight about a matter that's totally different. It's obvious you don't understand what I'm talking about. I'm happy to talk later with you individually, Yacoub. And I know you extracted yourself from the Manakh in a very timely manner." How could he know this?

And so the night went. I didn't understand until the very last of the evening when I learned Zain was discussing a project that would deal with currency trading. The subject was entirely esoteric to me.

Zain and Azar set upon me at the end of the evening. I was informed about the barest details of the project. I was then told to commit 100,000 KD to the effort. That amount, I was informed, was the smallest of the group. The other men who had attended seemingly knew the figure that was expected of them, and they were quite elated about the project. What was the hold they had on me? Why was I compelled to participate when I did not desire or understand?

Then, the course was made clear. "Yacoub, we need the funds your family is able to provide. The margin to be gained from currency trading is small and the only way to ensure large gains is to utilize a large pool of funds."

"But the decision is mine, of course."

"Of course it's your decision. But you must understand that not to participate could set in motion serious consequences."

"Oh, such as...?"

Azar interjected, "I'm familiar with the events you brokered in Arizona. You know what I am talking about, with your philandering. And then, I have heard about your thesis, the one no one has ever seen. Perhaps it should be widely read."

I rose from the gilded couch, promised to respond to their request, and gave the proper valedictions to gain exit. It was late and Rabea would be waiting, for she was eager for another child.

More than at any point in life I felt trapped by realities and not just by theoretical or theological concerns. And I knew nothing about the trading of currencies. And why was my participation even needed?

There was only one choice in seeking information about currency trading, John Friedecker. I could trust no one else to keep the necessary confidence. We met for a walk along the Gulf

Road, which was our favorite site. It was after sundown and the breeze was off the Gulf, and somewhere in the distance were the gunboats of the Iranian Navy, which were attempting to present themselves as a threat to Kuwaiti shipping.

"Why in the world have you developed an interest in currency trading? It's a black box. It's impossible to make money there unless you have vast resources and a lot of information."

"I've been led to believe we have what we need."

"By whom? Yacoub, as a friend, I want to caution you. It's really complicated."

"I don't mean any lack of confidence in our friendship, but I just can't tell you. It's best for you that I don't. And I've been assured of the success of the endeavor."

"There's no such thing as certainty in finance and economics. But I'll give an abbreviated lecture without the usual pedantics. Here's the 101 version: Free floating conditions in international currency trading began only about ten years ago, but the rules on trading have been different depending on the country. The shortened expression for the whole process is the Forex, for foreign exchange. You'll probably hear that term. But just remember that the rules of exchange differ from country to country. For example, Iran doesn't yet participate at all. The margin of profit, even with success, is low. One unit you need to know about is the PIP, which stands for Percentage in Point. Currency quotations are given in five significant figures. A PIP is the first digit on the right. For example, if the value in US dollars of one KD is 3.4712 dollars, and the US dollar rises to 3.4714, the value has risen 2 PIPs. That should give you an idea about the small changes that normally occur. So, in order for there to be a significant profit or loss, the change must be excessive or the amount of the investment very large. And of course, very large trades have the potential in themselves to influence the market.

"Traders use one of two general methods. The first has to do with mathematical modeling of trends. You have to know about trading level trends, Bollinger bands, Fibonacci analysis, and such. The second requires the knowledge of the way trends form, which could be helped by an awareness of certain events that are occurring either nationally or internationally."

The men I had met with didn't seem like mathematicians, so the latter method was more likely.

"But the thing to emphasize about both these methods is that neither possesses the element of certainly you referred to. The only way to approach certainty would be to have control or fore-knowledge of future events. If that knowledge were available, then the likelihood of success would rise. But then the specter of illegality or unethical behavior rises proportionally.

"For trading right now, the Kuwaiti dinar is linked to a weight-ed currency basket, which lessens the fluctuations in the market. The basket is made up of currencies from various countries in Europe. So, if you trade the dinar, you would buy into the cur-rency basket. This mixing of the currencies lessens the potential gain or loss to an even greater extent.

"Makes sense, doesn't sound complicated.'

"Just remember the Manakh. A lot of smart people thought they were in great shape. Currency trading is not as risky as the Manakh was, but unless you know what you're doing, I'd avoid it. Why in the world do you want to know about it?"

"John, you've been a big help. But I really don't think I should tell you about the specifics."

"You're scaring me a little. You know I want the best for you. You should be aware the Ministry of Finance tracks large cur-rency trades, and they have a link to the Kuwait security people. As a whole they aren't very efficient but a few of them are quite dedicated to their pursuit." It was dark now and we could hear the small waves lapping against the sea wall, and the ocean was brown against the night sky.

John finished the evening, "And Yacoub, I have to say what I think about this white camel business. I think you're being deceived by him."

I closed, "Don't insult me."

The next morning I left a brief note on Azar's desk: "I'm in. What's next?"

That afternoon Azar arrived at my office and shut the door behind him. "As I told you earlier, we will expect you to contribute 100,000 KD. As proceeds are accumulated, and they will be accumulated, they will be re-invested. When we deem that a satisfactory conclusion has been reached, you will receive back your 100,000 KD along with the profits accrued. We anticipate the term of the investment will be approximately two years."

"When will our group meet again? I need to learn about Bollinger bands and Fibonacci numbers and that sort of thing."

"I've never heard of those. Don't concern yourself about the technical aspects. And it's best we do not meet again as a large group. There may be get-togethers of several of us from time to time."

By now I was certain the actions of the group were not what I wanted to be involved in, but Azar's comments and their implication left no exit. I remembered John's warning about monitoring by the Finance Ministry, and I brought this up to Azar. "Every great endeavor has risk," left me with a cold feeling in the middle of my stomach. And the white camel had not visited for some time.

The next morning as I awoke the camel came, looked frightened, and ran into the dunes. The message was clear. I should have done the same.

All was quiet in Kuwait for two weeks. There were rumors, which spread at a rate only possible in Kuwait, of Iranian incursions into Kuwaiti territory, but nothing confirmed. Then, news sources reported Iranian jets bombing the Kuwaiti oil installation at Umm Al-Ayah, an Iranian response to Kuwait's support for Iraq. But rumors continued to build on the theory that the real culprits were Shia militants from Iraq and Lebanon.

The next day the Kuwaiti dinar fell precipitously against the European currency basket. Azar was beaming. He whispered to me, "We just made our purchase. You are now an owner of your country's currency."

Why had he not said 'our country'?

The next few weeks were quiet, and the dinar slowly but steadily recovered its value. Then, a brief encounter in the hall was punctuated by Azar's comment, "Today we sell." And there was no more explanation as we ate together in the school cafeteria, where the male and female faculty ate in the same room, but usually separated voluntarily by gender, and the students were totally segregated into different rooms. I was struck by the odd juxtaposition of international trading schemes, which I did not yet understand, and the highly traditional social setting.

Early the next morning we were awakened from sleep by a loud but distant explosion. We didn't know the origin until several hours later when the television news reported a Chinese-made Silkworm missile launched from an Iranian vessel had struck near one of the oil installations on the shore near Ahmadi. There were no injuries and minimal damage but had the Iranian aim been better, the damage might have been extensive. Reflecting international concern about Kuwait's resources, the dinar plummeted in international markets.

I sought out Azar later that day out of concern about the investment. His response, "Don't worry; we sold yesterday. We are in control of the situation. And today we bought back in, and at a very good price." I was pleased at the presentiment of the investment group, but surprised at their timeliness.

Weeks passed as the dinar recovered. Then, a Silkworm struck a Kuwaiti oil tanker, flagged by the US. The damage and loss of life this time were extensive. I learned the same series of events had occurred: a sale of the dinar holdings the day preceding the attack and a re-purchase at the nadir of the dinar value.

Azar suggested a small but discret celebration at the continuing good fortune of the investment group. Only it was not "good fortune." He invited Rabea and me down to his family's beach house south of Kuwait City. "Why don't you bring along John Friedecker and his family."

We proceeded down King Fahad bin Abdul Aziz Road past Al Khiran and turned left toward the beach at Nuwaiseeb just north of the entry point into Saudi Arabia. The road down to the turn-off was well paved but the occasional camel crossing and herders with sheep and goats often interrupted the way. The road became rough as we drove to the beach house, which was more modest than I expected. But the beach itself was exquisite: clean white sand with several large palms and clear water, not cloudy as near the city and oil depots.

We arrived simultaneously with the Friedeckers. The social milieu became quickly awkward, for there was a mix of gender and culture. The sexes were rescued and separated by Azar and his wife. Rabea sought to be by the side of John's wife, Rebecca. The women were taken away to a separate room indoors, and it was evident to Rebecca this would not be a true beach day for her.

* * *

At 8 PM as the sun was dissipating, the servants brought in several baked hamour with french fries and fruit, and the evening concluded shortly after. The women served themselves.

As we drove back to Ahmadi, Rabea was full of excitement at being able to talk with John's wife, Rebecca. "Yacoub, I felt such an immediate bond with Rebecca. Can't we have them over to out home for a meal?"

"I suppose you told her you became a believer in Jesus. You know how dangerous that could be for us."

"I told her. She understands the situation. I trust her."

* * *

The next months saw a series of coincidences that confirmed a repeating theme. The dinar always crept back up after its losses. Sales and repurchases occurred in a remarkably timely manner, draped around a disaster of some ilk. One afternoon Azar informed me they were selling the holdings. The next day an Iranian gunboat attacked and destroyed an offshore oil platform. The dinar obediently fell and a repurchase was made. Azar summoned me to a meeting at his home in the evening. There were only four attendees in total. We spoke casually, drank cardamom coffee, and the dinar purchase was mentioned only in passing. It had been clear for some time that the sequences of these events were not coincidental. I suspected the only real purpose of the meeting was to further implicate me in the events.

Once more the dinar rebounded over one month. The timely sale of the recovered currency was followed by an attack on the US and British Embassies. There was no loss of life but there was extensive structural damage to the buildings. The BBC reported Iranian Shia nationals had conducted the raids. They were not apprehended.

But John had been correct about the Ministry of Finance. The usually incompetent administration had taken great notice of the currency fluctuations punctuated by large blocks of timely sales and re-purchases based on the European currency basket. They traced the purchases to a Swiss firm, Imperator, Ltd., but the trail went dry at that point. So, the inspectors began systematically examining the records of virtually every wealthy family in the country. As head of the Al-Tamimi family they came to Suhayb. My politically astute and well-placed brother had no trouble assuring the men of the loyalty of our family. He opened the books available to himself. When they asked to see the financial records of my Kuwait Tool and Electrical Company, Suhayb's confident manner dissuaded them from proceeding out to Ahmadi. When I was informed of the investigation, I was able to conceal my fear, but I knew now that again the white camel been correct. The danger of what we were doing was real.

This time the recovery of the dinar value following the embassy attacks was slower than previously. The next sale did not occur for three months. And this time the trigger event was an attempted assassination of the Emir. Once again an Iranian Shia connection was suspected.

The fall in the dinar was precipitous and deep. Azar was gleeful at the price at which we were able to make the re-purchase. "Yacoub, we will be the richest men in Kuwait."

But given the national alarm over the near death of the Emir and the accumulation of the recurring attacks, the dinar did not resume its usual trajectory of recovery. Azar began to look worried because, with each of the cycles of fall and rise, the total amount of the original investment and all the profits were used for the re-purchase. A lack of recovery of the dinar would mean a substantial loss.

Then, as if anticipating the problem, a series of editorials began to appear in the Kuwait Times. These editorials were directed at the heart of the Kuwaiti economy and were filled with optimistic remarks. The main points addressed were the underlying strengths of the Kuwaiti dinar buttressed by oil and financial reserves, the fact that Allah protected the Emir, the wisdom of the Kuwaiti business community, and the spirit of the Kuwait people. A sample: "While we must acknowledge we have had many severe shocks in the last eighteen months, the strength of our State remains real. We possess immeasurable reserves of oil and solid backing for the dinar. The only reason for the dinar's recent decline is fear, not any logical reason. The Persians have

188 • JIM CARROLL

not cowed the Kuwaiti people, and we can demonstrate this fact to them by our national confidence. Mark my words, the Kuwaiti dinar will rise again." And it did.

Two months later, Kuwaiti evening news reported that large numbers of Shia of Iranian origin were being deported from Kuwait as a matter of national security. The deportees included many who had Kuwaiti citizenship. The estimates ran as high as 12,000. I phoned Azar's home; there was no answer. The next morning, I nearly ran to Azar's office. Papers were disheveled and the pictures and plaques on the wall had been removed. After my classes, I drove to Azar's house on Gulf Road. The Pakistani gateman was there. I used simple Arabic with the nonfluent gateman, "Wain Azar?" (Where is Azar?)

"Mu mujood." (not available) "Hallas." (finished)

The gateman allowed me to pass. The fountain was no longer flowing, and the water in the large collection basin was already green with algae. I proceeded to the double entry door. It was partially open, and I went into the entry area. The marble hall was dusty and some of the furniture was gone. There were no sounds of life in the house.

Two weeks passed and there was no word from Azar, and no money either. And the waiting was interrupted by another picture from Sattie along with a request for "college funds."

Then a note appeared on my desk at school.

> Dear Yacoub,
>
> I am sorry we had to depart so quickly. I know you understand as a friend. I thank you for assisting us in our endeavor. I will send 20,000 KD for your trouble. The political situation does not permit us to send more. You may pick up the draft at Maghreb Finance in the Global Tower on Al-Shuhada Street.

Your friend and colleague,

Azar

I was not surprised at the course of events. The 20,000 KD was a sad return on the original investment of 100,000 KD, and the profits must have been tremendous. Clearly, I would not share in them. By this time I knew why I had been involved. Azar had considerable information about my indiscretions, both religious and social. I had been brought on board to deflect the blame from himself and his colleagues.

I parked in the dusty lot in front of the Global building, and started to enter, but I saw two men who were inspectors from the Finance Ministry. Then, there were two more and accompanying them in handcuffs was the Times reporter who had written the series of editorials which served to strengthen the dinar. I got back in my car and drove away. I needed the money but not enough to risk arrest. Azar had set me up to be caught. What would the charge be? Treason? And somehow, I knew these troubles had arisen long ago from my foolish desire to know what I had not been able to know.

But perhaps I would know. Perhaps I should talk more with Rabea. The next evening I asked Rabea to go for drive down to the area near the Seif Palace on Gulf Road. Rabea sensed my continuing unease, "You seem more upset, especially since our trip to Nuwaiseeb and then even more as your friend Azar had to leave Kuwait. Tell me why you're troubled. The Bible, my book, tells me we are one."

I couldn't offer an adequate response.

The Grand Mosque of the State of Kuwait had just been completed, and we parked nearby and walked to the immense structure. The minaret dominated the outside of the building and was illuminated with gold-colored lamps. The attendant was asleep.

There were no worshippers, so we wandered in. The ceilings reached to heaven, and the arches were almost as high. The dominant colors were gold and pale blue. The open spaces within the building were large enough to accommodate thousands of worshippers, but tonight we were the only two.

"I should apologize for bringing you here. I know this is not for you anymore."

"No Yacoub, it's beautiful, and it was built to honor God. The building doesn't say anything more to me."

"And you're not threatened by the other messages of the building?"

"No, why should I be?"

"I envy you in this.'

"You needn't. I love you, Yacoub."

And as we drove back to Ahmadi we stopped for an ice cream cone at a shop where Rabea directed. We ordered chocolate, and the proprietor placed a plastic cover on the ice cream to protect from the dust before we reached the car.

The brief evening drive with Rabea was reassuring even though there was no substantive outcome.

But the political situation in the country continued to totter as the fear of Iran grew. This feeling was coupled with the Emir dissolving the National Assembly solely because some of the members had criticized members of the Cabinet. The Emir had perceived correctly that there was no allowance for open disloyalty. Kuwaiti shipping continued to be harassed by Iranian gunboats, but this was brought under control by the timely protection of both the Soviet Union and the US.

* * *

The Al-Faw peninsula extended south of Basra down to Umm Qasr on the west and Al-Faw on the east. The Kuwaiti possession of Bubiyan Island received the waters of the Tigris-Euphrates estuary south of the peninsula. For two more years the fighting went back and forth between Iranian and Iraqi forces. The ferocity for the extended battle was demonstrated by reports from senior Kuwaiti military officers stationed on Bubiyan. In the diwaniya I heard their descriptions of the feasting by the sharks as the blood and bodies floated round the island and out into the Gulf.

After eight years of bloody and pointless conflict, however, both Iran and Iraq had exhausted their physical and monetary resources. The war came to a reluctant conclusion in August 1988. Although there had been no gain of territory or wealth for either side, both declared victory. For a time the Gulf and Kuwait were at peace. But for me, conflicts only expanded.

CHAPTER 34

The Friedeckers

While I was not estranged from my parents, brother Suhayb and family, the time with them was awkward. Salman was now physically and mentally older than his actual age. He did not enter into the interactions. As Salman's wife, my mother had become a non-entity. The field was dominated by Suhayb who established himself both as a religious and business leader in Kuwait. I was jealous of Suhayb. How could this have happened to one inferior to me? Consequently, the time we spent with my family gradually diminished. Rabea, because her parents had been deported, had little contact with her family. All this settled well with Rabea.

And so the Friedecker family came to be frequent guests at our Ahmadi home, and similarly we often visited the Friedeckers in the block behind Mubarak Hospital home just off Tunis Street. The Friedecker family was large by Western standards. There were the eight-year-old twins, Evelyn and Gerta, six-year old Martha, the infant Ralph, and the oldest, twelve-year-old Andrew.

The dinners were unique for us. Only on family occasions did the men, women and children eat at the same table. Unrelated families usually separated men from the women and children during meals and other social occasions. But with the Friedeckers the presence of both John and Rebecca led a civility to the experience, which contributed to a convivial and relaxed atmosphere. John's children were polite and free to speak.

The times were a haven to Rabea, both in practicing her conversational English and for the fellowship with Rebecca. For my part, the relationship with John was one of the few where I could speak unguardedly. John displayed none of the concerns that plagued my conversations with family or Arab associates. And he was sensitive to my continuing disquiet about Islam and frankly any religion, so that he didn't push the issue.

"I'm in a maze, a maze that has no entry point and no exit. I wander from compartment to compartment with no hope of exit." Thus, I began as John and I sat together after dinner. In contrast to Arab custom, the time to stay and talk occurred after the meal. The children had been put to bed, and Rabea and Rebecca had coffee in the kitchen.

I respected John for his lack of pointless sympathy, and tonight he was no different. "Why do you think you are in such a place? Is it an accident, a plan of the 'great being,' or just your own doing?"

"Probably the latter."

"So you think you have sole responsibility for the way events pile up?" John was apparently in an unkind mood.

"No, of course not. You seem a bit irritated."

"I'm sorry, but it's always the same thing—it's that some one or some thing is opposing you, and you can't find the right way to undertake combat. Do you think there might be other possibilities?" John had already given his views on the "great being," and I did not see the sense in Christianity. I had encountered all that in Arizona. John had no intention to make the discussion a contest, and he changed the subject by a few degrees.

"How are the dreams?"

"I'm afraid to say it: they're confusing. There're basically two categories of dreams: the ones that occur in the middle of the night, and the ones after I wake up. I suppose you wouldn't call those dreams when I'm awake. The ones in the middle of the night are like stories. Often they're really entertaining, in fact so much so that I think I should write short stories based on them. If I wake, I go back to sleep thinking of the dreams so I can re-enter them. Sometimes I can. A few times I've gotten up and made notes. But then in the morning the notes aren't logical or as realistic as the dreams seemed at the time. Then the reality of these dreams fades quickly and what seemed like a great story becomes vacant in its essence. And finally there's nothing left of them. I can recall the pleasurable feeling they generated but not the content. The content is varied and covers everything, every feeling."

John didn't interrupt.

"There are dreams of a woman I knew in London when I was young. Her hair was brown and thick, and when she washed it, it smelled like the garden of the Emir on a warm night. And when I awake, I try to reclaim the odor by inhaling deeply, but it fails to return. But mostly, I don't dream of our time together. I dream about what became of her later on and of meeting her under new circumstances, when she has transformed into something I imagine. Then, for a brief time following the dream, it gives me plea-sure to ruminate about what the dream shows of her future. It has no relation, absolutely none, to reality.

"Of course there are the dreams characterized by some type of pursuit or attack. I'm being chased or attacked by a force, pur-sued to the point of violence. They still frighten me, and for time after I awake, they seem real. I may awaken during these. But everyone has dreams like these. We used to call them nightmares when I was little. For me then they were frequent. Suhayb never had them."

"What about the ones that come on after you wake up?"

"Your doctor friend from the US tried to cure me of those, but I wouldn't let him. They're important to me. Since I saw your friend I've read up on narcolepsy. I agree with his diagnosis from the medical standpoint. But the dreams after I awaken and can't move are distinctive and memorable. They don't fade. There's the white camel who rarely speaks but demonstrates certain things by his actions. I feel he's trying to lead me."

"Is the white camel always correct?"

"His actions aren't always clear enough for me to be sure. But the recurrent appearance of the camel over many years is a source of comfort."

"Then, why don't you have more assurance?"

"Sometimes, a lot of time passes between his visits."

"That's inconvenient."

"But I won't take the medicine that might banish him."

"I accept what you say about the camel but I don't understand. Maybe it's just a dream. And if it's not a dream, then the camel may be dangerous."

I responded, "I don't get it. What do you mean?"

"Don't be naïve. You must know about demons."

"The superstitious Bedouins speak of jinn. They're just a relic." Then I gave the standard medical response. "Actually the medical books call the dreams during waking a hypnogogic hallucination—not very complimentary to my psyche. But the camel is as real as your sitting here in front of me."

* * *

The conversation in the kitchen in Ahmadi was considerably more agreeable but not as happy. "Rebecca, I'm glad we have our times together. Since my neighbor in Ahmadi left I have only Divina that I can really speak with about what I believe. Yacoub says I must keep it to myself. And I know he's right. It could be dangerous, especially with the all the pressure Yacoub's been under. I think he's gotten into things he shouldn't have."

"I wish you could go the NECK with us."

"It's not possible."

"Or perhaps you could meet with me and a group of women here in our home."

"No, there's too much risk. I know you want what's best for me, but you don't understand."

* * *

The spring of 1989 came with enough rain to generate a green blanket in portions of the desert, and I had my employees set up a black tent in the desert near Ahmadi but away from the oil fields. Rabea, Hibah and I spent several days on weekends in the tent. Before the days turned uncomfortably warm, we asked the Friedeckers to join.

The Friedeckers brought with them an additional child, Rania. We weren't prepared. The Friedeckers had taken the severely impaired child out of the Mubarak children's ward. The story of Rania, the child of poor Palestinian parents, was sadly typical of such situations in Kuwait, recognized as a societal problem by many but acknowledged as important by few.

We sat quietly while Rebecca told the story. "Rania was one of twins. The twins were prematurely born at Maternity Hospital. Rania's twin brother was larger and more vigorous at two kilos, while Rania had weighed only 1.6 kilos. Her brother went home first to be among his four siblings. The father had only part-time work, and the new son was more than they needed. Consequently, when Rania came ready for discharge from Maternity, the family didn't appear. Weeks passed and still the parents did not come to the hospital for their child. Finally, the hospital authorities summoned the police to fetch the parents, and they capitulated by taking Rania. Even under the care of the hospital nurses, Rania hadn't thrived, but in the crowded, poor home there was little chance for Rania. The next contact she had with the medical facilities was her first admission to Mubarak for dehydration and 'failure to thrive,' as it's clumsily called. Once again, the parents delayed in accepting the child after her discharge. On her next admission to Mubarak Rania was more seriously ill. She was admitted through the emergency department with vomiting and dehydration. A Filipino nurse saw that Rania was not using her right side. A CAT scan was done, and there was a fractured skull and large blood clot on the left side of her brain. The neurosurgeon operated, and the procedure was partially successful. Rania survived but with brain damage. She was also found to have fractures of her forearm, ribs, and femur.

"They don't accept the idea of battered children in Kuwait. The Mubarak hospital authorities didn't know how to deal with the matter. The Kuwaiti doctors said, 'Child abuse does not occur in Kuwait.' They didn't know how to take legal action on behalf of the child against the parents. If the child were removed from the family, who would take care of her? And now that Rania was brain damaged, would anyone want her? Once again the same series of events occurred and once again the abuse was repeated after the issue was forced upon the family. There was no solution for Rania with the parents. The father had no papers and worked only intermittently. Their living quarters were inadequate, and there was barely enough food for the healthy. Rania was expendable, and her healthy twin was a boy. She was admitted again to Mubarak with a two-kilogram weight loss. This time there was agreement among the staff that the child could not be discharged to the parents. The mother began to visit the hospital with some regularity. But her purpose wasn't Rania. She developed a relationship with two male hospital security guards. The outcome was tolerated among the hospital personnel. The mother would visit the child briefly and then receive whatever benefit she could from the guards, sexual and that which was needed by the family, the money for her services.

"We finally became involved as a family. The same Filipino nurse who had recognized Rania's arm weakness told Rania's story during our Sunday school class at the NECK. I began to visit the child on the ward. Sometimes our children went along with me. After a time the nursing staff knew them and their presence was tolerated even though they had no right to visit Rania. Andrew often went to Rania's bedside to assist with what he called physical therapy.

"I asked the hospital social worker for permission to take Rania into our home, first on weekends, and then more and more often. The hospital finally granted permission in writing. We knew that, for a Muslim child to be allowed to be taken by Christians into their family, even on a temporary basis, was a miracle in itself."

Even Rabea was uncomfortable with the arrangement. Perhaps there would be retribution. But Rabea came to embrace the idea, and she had the driver take her to the Friedecker home in order to assist with the care of Rania while Rebecca conducted home school with the Friedecker children. Rabea and Rania became friends.

For six months the arrangement persisted. While the Rania issue did not interfere with the day-to-day aspects of my life, I remained confused about the meaning of the events. I saw in them as intrinsic failure of Islam. In this context, how is it that Islam would not have a means to help a helpless child? And further, what is the position of Islam in regard to the injustice inflicted on Rania?

The Friedecker family's growing love for Rania culminated in the desire to take the child into their family officially. The discussion of adoption was broached with the hospital social worker. It was here the boundary was reached. First, the concept of full adoption is foreign in Islam. While it would not be unusual that a Muslim family would take in a needy child, the idea of equality with the natural children was unheard of in practical or Quranic terms. But the roadblock was this: a Christian family could not adopt a Muslim child.

Such was my discouragement with Islam. But perhaps there was another alternative. The Friedeckers could convert to Islam. Rabea's response was, "They will refuse." I couldn't understand how she was so sure.

The Friedeckers rejected this solution out of hand. I was amazed at their recalcitrance. What, after all, was the point of religion, if not to care for the weak? Does a vacant principle supersede justice?

So, by my analysis, Rania was cast off by both Islam and Christianity. All religions had failed Rania.

* * *

My religious deconstruction continued at an accelerated rate. Unlike nominal Muslims, or nominal partakers of any religion, who could put their system aside like a heavy garment on a warm day, I was faced with the necessity of actually teaching Islam as a subject to young students. My assigned classes for the second semester of the school year were The Transmission of the Quran in Historic Context, The Hadiths as Instruments of Allah, and Forms of Islamic Jurisprudence. The first two courses were required of freshmen and sophomore students of several related disciplines. The interest of the students in these two courses was lackluster at best, and their desultory attitudes contributed to my pain. I had to seem sincere in order to teach the courses, and the effort drained my spirit of any remaining security in Islam. Occasionally, one of the better students would ask a penetrating question. Was the inquisitor seeking to expose me?

The jurisprudence course was for more advanced students. For this topic, it was possible for me to hide in the details of the complex subject. In an area where I was far more knowledgeable about minutia, I could preempt questions and leave the class lost in the morass. I thought the semester would never end. When June finally arrived, I was exhausted from the self-betrayal.

Even the weather had abandoned me. Early June was marked by a series of *toz* [Kuwaiti Arabic for sand storms] that clouded the daytime sky with a sun-obscuring yellow haze. At night the dust was choking and discouraging. The Kuwait weather reports called it *Al-Bawareh*. Was this a message from Allah?

But it was also in June 1989 that Rabea announced her pregnancy. Yes, I was happy for her, but mystified at Rabea's continuing exultation in virtually every aspect of life. Even the promise of new life did not enhance my expectation of what was to come. Without the hope I had formerly possessed about finding the solution in Islam, I couldn't muster delight. Rabea was aware of my loss of moorings. Certainly John knew, and I was saddened by John's lack of sympathy in this state.

At fifty-one, I looked in the mirror and saw a gaunt and gray-bearded figure. Although I had spent little time in the desert, I could be mistaken for an old Bedouin with hawk nose and droopy eyelids. The years of seeking Islam had not been kind.

CHAPTER 35

A New Venture

The Islam classes at the university dragged me down, and I therefore resolved to resign.

To fill the gap, I embarked on a new business arrangement through my Kuwait Tool and Electric Company operating out of Ahmadi, and the negotiation of the contracts required that I drive periodically north to Basra. I traveled up Highway 80 to the bordertown of Safwan. Just before Safwan I crossed the highest point in Kuwait, the rocky escarpment of the Mutlaa ridge, and then on to Basra, the City of Palms.

The ending of the Iran–Iraq war in August 1988 and the needed rejuvenation of southern Iraq had paved the way for his venture. The signs of battle were still evident. There were burned out Soviet T-54 and T-55 tanks, and the roadway itself was in need of repair from the grooves made by the tank travel. I stayed in a small hotel near the river and met with an Iraqi, Abdul Josef, who was seeking to serve as an intermediary to purchase whatever equipment I could supply. At first the expressed need was for re-establishing the work of the southern Iraq oil fields, an area where I could supply the necessary apparatus. Initial discussions took place in the hotel.

Then, Abdul Josef asked me to his home for dinner, and of course, an acceptance was required. The dinner featured a large, baked fish from the Tigris-Euphrates estuary. The freshwater fish was distinctive in taste and more delicate than the saltwater fish from the Gulf. But rather than the usual departure soon after the meal, we adjourned into another room, and I came aware that more was expected from his visit. The discussion turned to other materials I might provide along with the oil equipment. The materials, unspecified, would arrive at the Kuwait harbor at Shuwaikh, inspection would be minimal, which would be assured by necessary fees to the inspectors, and the materials would then be loaded onto the truck with the oil equipment. Inspection at the border would be cursory. The amount paid for each shipment would be 50,000 KD, in addition to the amount for the oil drilling equipment. I accepted the lucrative offer without questioning the contents of the shipment arriving from abroad.

The shipments proceeded as stated. Two shipments per month were scheduled in the beginning and after six months increased to three per month. Their timing was controlled by the arrival of cargo at Shuwaikh rather than the availability of drilling equipment or its requirement in Basra. My direct involvement was no longer required as my drivers conducted the pickups, transport and deliveries. One of the experienced drivers reported to me that the materials at Shuwaikh were offloaded from a Chinese freighter line. More concerning was the driver's report that the designations on the crates were spray-painted out as they were transferred to the truck. The truck was then loaded with the drilling equipment on top of the crates. The regular transfer of 50,000 KD to the Kuwait Tool and Equipmment Company softened my apprehension. The payments originated from the Rasheed Bank in Baghdad, which had just been established in the prior year, 1988. Abdul Josef's name was not attached to the fund transfer. The drilling equipment was paid for separately by an account in Basra under Abdul Josef's name. By the time of the birth of the expected child in January 1990, I had increased my personal wealth by means of the shipments.

Rabea delivered at Maternity Hospital, January 1990, and I finally had the son, Yusef, who would remain in my home. Rabea's aunt came to the hospital only briefly, but Rebecca Friedecker was there the entire time and drove Rabea and the baby back to our home in Ahmadi. Her elation over the new child and a friend she could rely on contributed to her contentment. The fact I was involved with business and at odds with myself did not diminish her happiness. I knew I was neglecting my wife and family, and I couldn't understand Rabea's tolerance of this state. That Rabea loved me remained a puzzle.

In April 1990 Abdul Josef came to Kuwait to meet me. While he was staying in the International Hotel, however, he was arrested by the Kuwait Secret Service and taken to the Central Prison. I was afraid to help.

Yet the shipments continued, and so did the money deposits. I did not even know whom to contact to end the arrangement. Apparently it had been necessary to compartmentalize the participants in the plan such that if Abdul Josef was removed from the picture, the process could not be terminated. There was no one to bring it to a close. I couldn't stop a train of events. I awaited the arrival of the police but they never came. Rabea sensed my chagrin, but accepted it as part of my make up. It was like a long illness.

Then in early summer of 1990 news came from the Northern Iraqi city of Jalala that the population had been devastated, perhaps as many as 5000 people lost due to their being attacked by Saddam with poison gas. It was said to be sarin. The UN was summoned to the site to take samples. Within two months it was published in the Kuwaiti newspapers that the sarin had been made in China. The speculation centered on how the shipment had been completed. I thought I knew.

By July 1990 the shipments stopped. The shipments simply stopped appearing, no notice was given. Was there really a connection between the gas and the transport from China to Iraq? I told myself the connection was not certain.

By the summer of 1990 I was distraught. First, there was the joy of six-month-old Yusef, who by now was interactive and, as Rabea said repeatedly, daddy's boy. Second, there was Rabea, whose demeanor and love for me surpassed anything I could hope for. But there was the loss of academic connection. I regretted the loss of status, and my position in the diwaniya fell. But the worst was the haunting news from Jalala, with the sarin gas and the death of the 5000 people.

I expected the police or security forces to appear at my door. I would have been relieved. Was I protected by Salman's status or by family name? Or was it simply the inefficiency of the system?

The concealed theft by my Kuwait Tool and Electric Company of earlier years, the currency investments, and the dubious shipments to Iraq, all of which had made my personal financial condition exceed anything I had imagined, should have been a comfort financially. But I was never free.

CHAPTER 36

Summer 1990

As 1990 progressed I spent more time at home with Rabea and the two children. My visits to the diwaniya lessened. There were times when even Rabea showed impatience with my moroseness.

And there were rumors of unresolved discussions between Kuwait and Iraq. I dismissed these concerns. Kuwait had aided Iraq during the recent war, and there was no reason for worry.

But there were recurring trips back and forth between the foreign ministers of Iraq and Kuwait over the ensuing months. I watched the TV reports, which showed the men smiling, seated, and nodding agreement. But was there a reason for the nodding? The Iraqi war debt to Kuwait was $14 billion. Iraq couldn't pay, and Kuwait wouldn't forgive.

Issam Chalabi, the Iraqi oil minister, argued that Kuwait was depressing the income from Iraqi oil by producing in excess of OPEC limits. Kuwait persisted in their elevated production levels and the price of oil declined accordingly.

The discussion then shifted to the Rumaila oil field of northern Kuwait near the Iraqi border. The area had been in border dispute for over thirty years. The Iraqi minister, Tariq Azziz, accused the Kuwaitis of taking advantage of our advanced drilling techniques and slanting their wells into Iraqi oil lands. To the embarrassment of all participants, arguments erupted in the Gulf Cooperation Council between the representatives of the two countries. After all, it was said, "We are brothers of the Arab Nation." The Kuwaiti news stations reported the favorable negotiations. Really?

By July the temperatures of 125 F had set upon Kuwait in full force, and those that could depart did so for cooler regions, as was their usual practice. In the evenings when the less fortunate residents took to the streets for their shopping, the heat sapped their breath as they emerged from their air-conditioned villas and apartments. We had decided not to travel abroad that year because of the new baby. But despite the summer quiet in Kuwait, the situation between the two countries was hopeless. Iraq would not pay and Kuwait would not forgive.

The Kuwaiti TV news stations continued their reports but their actual content was less informative than usual. August brought no relief from the heat or the diplomatic impasse. Western news stations reported that Iraq troops were positioned at the Kuwait border and in apparent battle formation. The Kuwaiti papers were devoid of such news. The Bedouins knew the Dog Star would soon rise to herald the fearful dawn.

At 2 AM on the morning of August 2, we were awakened from sleep by low-flying jets and explosions. Helicopter gunships strafed strategic sites. Four Republican Guard divisions, 1st Hammurabi Armored, 2nd al-Medinah al-Munawera Armored, 3rd Tawalkalna ala-Allah Mechanized Infantry, and the 4th Nebuchadnezzar Motorized, crossed the border in rapid order and overwhelmed Kuwaiti defensive positions.

The response of the Kuwaiti military was mixed. Most fought bravely but other units, staffed by third-world expatriots and *bidoons* (those without country identification) abandoned their positions and left flanks exposed. The end therefore came quickly, but the result would have been the same in any case. The Kuwaiti forces were outnumbered by a ratio of ten to one. While the Emir fled south to Saudi Arabia, the Emir's brother, Sheik Fahad, died attempting to defend the Dasman Palace. Due to its location near the sea, the palace was especially vulnerable to the attack by the Iraqi Marine landing.

* * *

Suhayb responded as the hero he was. Why couldn't I do the same? Suhayb's first consideration was the protection of Salman and Fatima and his own wife and children. The only realistic course for him was to confine them to the large house and compound. After the initial attack, the Iraqis did not invade private residences, as their first objective was to pacify the population and portray themselves as liberators. By August 3 there were only scattered pockets of Kuwaiti troops who fought on.

Suhayb realized the Iraqis were establishing complete control of the city. He therefore set about contacting his closest circle, which was comprised of other religious leaders and valued business associates. He achieved this by sending his non-Kuwaiti servants bearing verbal messages. He was concerned that the phones, when they were working, were subject to eavesdropping. Suhayb was the clear leader.

Meanwhile the Iraqis endeavored to bring about political control as the military forces were seeking out all corners of the large city. Alaa Hussein Ali of Iraq was named prime minister of Kuwait and Ali Hassan al-Majid (known as "Chemical Ali" for his efforts in gassing the Kurds) became the governor.

For Suhayb to see these individuals on Iraqi-controlled Kuwait TV attempting to sound Kuwaiti was a farce. Adding to the insult, the men were unable to wear the Kuwaiti gutra and iqal with the typical jaunty Kuwaiti style.

The need for the appearances of these two men was brief. Kuwait was soon annexed as part of Iraq. The justification for this move was the sensible duplicity of earlier Kuwaiti rulers who had allowed their country to become a British protectorate while never succeeding from the Ottoman Empire.

Suhayb waited out the initial flurry of activity and secured his collaborators. In the process of collecting information, one of his men, who was a contractor for the Kuwaiti army, located a cache of light arms that had not been found by the Iraqis. After dark the weapons were distributed among those who felt they could manage them. Any sort of frontal attack on the Iraqi military was out of the question, but brief attacks at night on Iraqi sentries became the style of harassment. The foreign news media dubbed the Kuwaiti shooters as the "resistance," which was considerably more romantic than realistic.

But the cost to the shooters and their families was high. Some were apprehended in the act, for they were not skilled in their chosen endeavor. And then, if they were not killed immediately, they were tortured to obtain information about their families, who were then taken prisoner and executed as collaborators. The information the Iraqis learned about the other members of the "resistance" was limited, as Suhayb had taken care to compartmentalize them into small cells.

The "resistance" continued into September and most of October. Its highlight was Suhayb's orchestration of the car bombing of the International Hotel adjacent to the US Embassy. A car laden with a bomb was driven into the covered car park in front of the hotel. This car park was designed as a part of the hotel itself with the hotel overhanging the driveway. The car was detonated remotely and, because it was parked with other vehicles in a close line, the gas tanks of the other vehicles were ignited in series. The result was quite effective with the blasts disrupting the entry area of the hotel itself. Several Iraqi officers including one brigadier general were killed, and there were many injuries of other Iraq officials who were occupying the former luxury hotel.

Suhayb had to admit that, while the effort was a success in itself, it accomplished nothing from a military standpoint and only resulted in a crackdown on upper level Kuwaiti families who might possibly have been involved. The punishments doled out in retribution were indiscriminate but effective in reducing the efforts of the resistance. Suhayb felt responsible for the Iraqi response. His sincerity in this, however, served to enhance his image in the community. He was, after all, a real patriot.

Suhayb was deflated by the lack of effect of his efforts but he turned them to other areas. He organized the food distribution in the community and set up communications with the Iraqi military in order to preserve some level of safety. Here, he was cleverly cooperative and thereby maintained the safety and value of his position. He awaited a better time.

* * *

While Suhayb and the resistance carried on their activities, I brooded in our Ahmadi house. I isolated our little family and felt estranged from the rest of the family and Kuwaiti community. Suhayb contacted me and asked me to join the fight for independence, but I declined. Suhayb said he understood. Suhayb still continued to phone and check on our needs and safety, and his magnanimity embarrassed me.

Although the international phone lines had been cut, the local phone system continued to function. There was the suspicion that the Iraqis monitored the content of calls, but realistically there was no way they could accomplish this for all the phone traffic. Even so, I was afraid whenever Suhayb phoned, but the primary reason for his frequent contacts was to make sure my family had sufficient food.

At night the Iraqis fired artillery, which was as much felt as heard. Suhayb informed me Iraq's arsenal included a variety of arms acquired from other nations: Austrian GHN-45s, South African G-5 155mm howitzers, and large numbers of older Soviet and Chinese guns. Was I responsible for any of those, thanks to my lucrative shipping operation?

On the evening of October 24, the artillery was particularly active, and we were unable to sleep. Loud knocking at our door at 11 PM raised me from our bed. Two Iraqi soldiers greeted me. And they were not soldierly.

I found the two men penitent rather than aggressive. "Can we come in and have something to eat?" They avoided eye contact.

I had no choice and allowed them to enter. The older soldier, Latif, was unshaven and overweight. He moved slowly and when seated at the table, a continuous resting tremor was visible. I had seen Parkinson's disease before and recognized it in Latif. Yusef, the younger, was thin and pale with a beard in its infancy.

Rabea, who had observed them from the bedroom, saw they were no threat, covered her head, entered the kitchen, and began to warm some lentil soup. She soon delivered the bread and thick soup along with tea to the men seated at the dining room table. Still, the men avoided eye contact while they ate.

Finally, I spoke, "Why are you here?"

Latif: "They don't bring us food or water regularly. We're hungry. And we don't want to fight."

After assuring us no harm was intended, the men explained themselves in more detail. Latif, at forty-seven, was actually much younger than his apparent age. He had fought for years, or rather accompanied the fighters, in the long war against the Iranians. Even though the neurologic disease now disabled him, his forced conscription had continued and he was stationed to guard the Ahmadi oil fields. Yusef, at sixteen, was more a boy than a soldier. He ate quickly and never looked up. He was the youthful image of fear itself.

They departed as quietly as they had come, and we went back to bed. Only Rabea slept. I was frustrated with her for her ability to sleep in the face of having had Iraqi soldiers for a meal.

The two returned every few days for a total of five visits, each for food and in the late evening when they were slated to be on guard duty. Their visits informed me of the sad state of the Iraqi army. Apparently few wanted to be in Kuwait. The Republican guard was distributed strategically to keep order among the common troops, who were poorly armed and fed, and discouraged.

On their fifth visit, as we were warming to the visitors and confident no harm was meant, two muffled rifle shots interrupted the meal, one through the front room window and another nearly simultaneously through the dining room window. Latif and Yusef slumped over the dinning room table each with blood streaming from head wounds. Rabea gasped and as she did so there was loud knocking on the front door. I imagined the Republican guard would accuse us of harboring soldiers who were supposed to be on duty.

But the soldiers at the door were not Iraqi. There were five muscular young men with camouflage uniforms and dark face paint. They were American, most likely Special Forces. The senior officer told the other four to clean up the blood and two bodies, and then he turned to me.

"You are Yacoub Al-Tamimi."

"Yes, that's correct."

"You are the owner of the Kuwait Electric and Tool Company?"

"I am."

"I understand your company provided shipping services from the Shuwaikh port to Iraq. That's why we're here. We need the information you can provide. You must tell us the truth."

I was undone.

"Do you know the contents of the shipments?"

"I never actually saw the shipments."

"Who provided the shipments?"

"I understand the freighters were Chinese."

"What did your men tell you about the manner in which the shipments were loaded? Was there an attempt at concealment?"

By this time my face was numb. "I'm not sure what you're asking."

"The shipments contained sarin gas made in China. Don't tell us you didn't know. We need to know the number of shipments and the capacity of the trucks that were used. We need to know, as accurately as possible, the amount of sarin Iraq has at its disposal. We know that some of the gas has already been used in Iraq."

"Yacoub, how could you, all those poor people in Jalala!" Rabea said. She began to cry and then her cries became gasps.

I went to the study and found the paperwork for the shipments. The Americans took them and put them in a brown plastic pouch. They then placed Yusef and Latif in black body bags and three of the men left quickly carrying the bodies. The two youngest Americans were left to clean the dining room, a task they accomplished with great facility. The marble floor lent itself to the task. The linen dining room tablecloth, however, was irreparably bloodstained, so they took it with them. It had been a wedding gift from Rabea's mother.

Rabea cried through the night. I was silent. There was nothing I could say. *Perhaps some of her tears were for Latif and Yusef and not for what I had done.*

CHAPTER 37

What's Left for Me

During the six months of the occupation, the Iraqis lost no opportunity to move the wealth of Kuwait back to Iraq. From the beginning until the conclusion it could be argued based on the northward movement of goods that the Iraqis never intended to remain in Kuwait.

Through all this, the looting, the torture, the reports of torture, the unending days of waiting for news of news, the visitation of the two Iraqi soldiers who were not to survive the war and American Special Forces, I waited. We were able to live in relative comfort, as Suhayb's men supplied us with food. The Ahmadi area, with its oil, was highly prized and therefore well guarded and little subject to looting. But I knew the US was aware of my role with Iraq, and now I wondered what the Iraqis knew.

And the white camel returned with regularity. I had not been troubled by the episodes of unexpected sleep or early morning paralysis for some time, but the anxious lassitude imposed by the occupation aggravated the malady.

The white camel seemed to call me to a city, not Kuwait City. The camel's lack of concern for my family disarmed me.

The answer was fulfilled by information brought by Suhayb, who made a high-risk visit to Ahmadi.

The conversation took place outside the garden, which had not received the usual irrigation. "Yacoub, you were visited by soldiers." It was a statement, not a question.

"Yes, there were two poor, forlorn Iraqi soldiers who came by several times."

"Not them, the Americans. I know about the visits of both the Iraqi soldiers and the American soldiers."

"But how..."

"The Americans are still here in Kuwait. They're working with the resistance. The Iraqis are fools. They don't understand what they've done and what it will cost them. But my concern for now is not the Iraqis. They will get what they deserve. My concern is for you."

I had no response.

"The Americans told the resistance you collaborated with the Iraqis."

"But it was before they invaded. I didn't know."

"Do you think that matters." Once again, it was a statement, not a question. "Yacoub, I know the men in the resistance. They're going kill you. In their eyes, you're a traitor."

"What should I do?"

"You must leave Kuwait. We'll watch over Rabea and the children."

Again, I must follow the white camel into betrayal. How easy Suhayb made it for me.

Suhayb left for the city. Now I had to tell Rabea. But before I could do so, Rabea cried out in desperation over the news bought by their Filipino maid, Divina. Rania had once again been brought to Mubarak. This time she could not be saved. The neglect and abuse finished her. Neighbors had found her in a closet and brought her to the emergency department, but there was nothing they could do or could have done in the best of times. Rania's death became emblematic of the failures of Islam, or indeed in any religion. I no longer had cause to maintain my honor.

So in the midst of an occupying army, I left my wife and children in order to preserve myself. The last vestige of Islam was vanquished from seeking or longing.

I told Rabea. She was still stunned by the news of Rania's death, and the need for my departure added to her sadness. But she agreed there was no choice. She would stay with Divina.

Suhayb would watch over her. He sent several of his men to take strategic positions in the neighborhood, which was now mostly abandoned. Suhayb assisted in planning my escape. I was amazed at the control and authority he had come to possess. Suhayb's pride of his younger years had been replaced by a quiet, admirable confidence. Suhayb's Islam was his bulwark. His faith was buoyant and unquestioning.

The Bedouins came for me in a jeep at nine in the evening. They had scouted the way out over the desert in order to avoid the Iraqi entrenchments, which at this point in late December were widespread and a puzzle to solve. But it was only about sixty kilometers to Wafra near the border, and within several hours we were across the Saudi border. We proceeded over to the coast road and down to Al Jubayl, where the Saudi forces were embedded. After the Saudis reviewed my documents, the Bedouins headed back north and I hired a car to take me to Riyadh, where I took a room for several days to determine if I could access my overseas financial account.

I recalled my happy, experimental days at university in London and resolved to re-inhabit my old domain in hopes of recapturing something. I wasn't sure what. I went to Taif, where the Emir was huddled with subordinates, and then to Jeddah, where the presence of the Americans was already striking. They were everywhere and blending in poorly. The female soldiers were uncovered. I booked a plane to London.

After I landed, I headed for central London on the Thames and the area around Kings College, where I rented a flat. Kuwaitis, many of whom had been outside the country when the Iraqis invaded, were scattered all over London. I avoided them.

The college and its environs had changed little in the thirty years since I had been there. It was several more days before I returned to the Red Lion. I ordered dark ale at the bar and tried to recall what had really occurred there.

The barkeeper engaged me after my second draft. "I don't know you, but you act like you've been here."

"I don't think much has changed. But it was a long time ago. I'm not sure what I remember – it's all jumbled up."

On my third visit to the pub, the conversation came alive. "You seem to be looking for someone."

"It's really been too long—thirty years. I'm sure there's no trace."

"No trace of what?"

"Of her, of course. It's always her, isn't it."

"Of course."

"Her name was Anna, a dark-headed woman. She's about my age."

"People around here tend not to leave. You might try the little bookshop over at Tavistock Street about three blocks from here. She could be the one you're looking for. That's her son over in the back booth."

I looked hard at the man, young but still too old to be a student. Perhaps he was thirty. His hair and skin were dark. I thanked the barkeeper and left for the evening.

I restrained myself as long as I could, but two days later I surrendered and headed for Tavistock. It was now late December, Christmas decorations were around the city, and it was cold and raining. The bookshop had the warm, pleasant mustiness of old books and little casual traffic. In addition to the new volumes, there were choices of rare books. An original copy of *Leaves of Grass* caught my eye and I opened it to the passage that read:

"Not I, nor anyone else can travel that road for you.

You must travel it by yourself.

It is not far. It is within reach.

Perhaps you have been on it since you were born, and did not know.

Perhaps it is everywhere—on water and land."

Anna had carved a niche as a rare book dealer. I envied the endeavor, one that appealed to me as a refuge. There was no one else in the store. Then I saw her behind the cash register bent over another old book. Her hair was flecked with gray and her pale skin had not weathered well, but there was no doubt. She still owned a rough, sexual demeanor.

"How much is this Whitman volume?"

She looked up and knew immediately. "I know you can afford it, and I know you'll pay my price." Perhaps there was a little smile, but I wasn't certain.

"Yes, whatever your price."

"I thought I'd never see you again. Adam brought me money after you left, but I never used it. You have a son."

"I know. I saw him at the Red Lion. I don't know what to say, except thank you for not doing what I intended."

"What are you doing here?"

"It's a long story. I had to get out of Kuwait."

"So, you're still running away again. I think it's best you don't speak with our son."

And that exchange was the end of it. I suggested we go to the Red Lion for a beer. Anna declined. I paid for the book and went out into the rain. I couldn't return to the Red Lion, so I found another pub on Milford Lane.

By the beginning of January it appeared the international community led by the US would finally take action against Iraq. Communication with Kuwait was difficult but on January 15 came the news the Iraqis had killed Suhayb, as a leader of the resistance. After all Suhayb had done for Rabea and me, I was at a loss as to how I should feel. All my life I had competed with Suhayb, first for our father's attention, and later for the praise of the community. Suhayb always won. Now there was no possibility of my competing with Suhayb, hero of the Kuwaiti resistance, in death. Suhayb achieved the final victory.

* * *

Rabea and the children remained cloistered with Divina in the house in Ahmadi. By this time there were no other families left on the block. Suhayb's men continued in their assignment and periodically brought food after dark, skillfully avoiding the Iraqi soldiers guarding the location.

Rabea focused on the Gospel of John and Paul's letter to Romans. By now Rabea was fluent in the English Bible, and Rabea and Divina were each a teacher of the other. Our two children were taught, as they were able to understand.

One evening in early February, Iraqi soldiers came for the sole purpose of looting the homes. The US air bombardment was now regular and increasingly effective as Special Forces already on the ground located Iraqi troop positions. Rabea's block, I was told, was granted a special dispensation by the Kuwaiti resistance, and the home was left untouched.

In late February, the desert spring came and with it the departure of the Iraqis. The resistance sent word to me that US and British ground forces had executed a rapid advance from the west rather than the south, where it had been expected. The Iraqi troops were overwhelmed in rapid order. News networks reported the slaughter on Mutlaa Ridge, where the Iraqis had intended to make a defensive stand. There were the later photographs of the carnage on the road north to Basra.

Upon the departure of the Iraqis from Ahmadi, they set fire to the oil wells, and the area quickly became uninhabitable. The US troops arrived and Rabea and Divina and the children were moved to the International Hotel, which had been the hostel for Iraqi officers during the occupation. They were able to look down upon the vacant US Embassy. Their stay in the hotel lasted a month. They took their meals in the hotel dining room buffet along with other Kuwaiti families needing refuge. Communication was now possible with me, and I planned my return. The remaining elements of the resistance had declared an unofficial amnesty for those Kuwaitis who had departed Kuwait under trying conditions. Rabea could only hope I was included. She had already forgiven me for my escape.

* * *

I took a jet to Jeddah and then traveled the rest of the way by car. The road north from Al-Jubayl was heavily damaged by the tank traffic, and it did not improve as I crossed the Saudi border at Nuwaiseeb. I asked the driver to go over to the beach where I found the cottages either destroyed or ransacked. The formerly pleasant beach and clear, shallow water were now stained by oil. I didn't know where to find Rabea so I went to my parents' home where I received a shallow greeting. Both my father and mother were older than I remembered, which I hoped was the explanation for their desultory reception. There was a large photograph of Suhayb on the main wall in the living room. A wilted rose adorned the picture. My first thought about the photo was that Suhayb would have said it was *haram* (forbidden).

Our family's farash took me to the house where Rabea, Divina, and the children were lodged, having moved from the hotel. The large house on Jasim Boodai Street was on loan while the owners remained in London. I was afraid Rabea's reception would be cold, and I prepared for this, but when I opened the gate and entered the garden, she ran, jumped, and clung to my neck, crying. Her hair was not covered, and the smell of it was overwhelmingly refreshing, freshly washed but oddly with a draft of charcoal. She couldn't stop crying for a time, but finally she took me by the hand and led me into the two children, who were uncertain about their returning, absentee father. Divina had prepared a dinner of fish over the charcoal grill, and its aroma evoked a deluge of memories—of afternoons on the beach at Nuwaiseeb, of childhood in the desert, and most of all, of the new memory of Rabea's hair.

As we began again as a family, Rabea informed me about the events in the city, but her emphasis was on how little they had actually been affected. I didn't understand at first that she was restraining herself from telling what God had done for her and Divina. But finally she was unable to hold back, and the reports of God's goodness came out. She was effusive in her praise. My interpretation was that the reported events and feelings were merely the gift of circumstance. I was neither Muslim nor Christian nor anything else that called itself a religion.

Within two weeks the city began to resurrect itself. Businesses re-opened. Fresh goods began to arrive in the country. The auto dealers ordered large numbers of vehicles, new and used. Banks re-opened, and I was able to secure access to my ample funds and purchase a new Mercedes. Slowly, I began to initiate contact with acquaintances.

My homecoming was not that of a hero. Like many other Kuwaitis who had either been outside Kuwait when the invasion began or who had departed under perceived threat, I was relegated to a lesser social class, not economically based, but rather in terms of the new brand of patriotism, which swept the city. And in that lower class, as one who had left during the occupation, I was in the lowest rank. As an Arab man who had left his family, there was little hope for social redemption. The network of horizontal reporting among the citizenry had not been damaged by the war, and my misdeeds were soon known.

Officials at the university met and I was called to a meeting in a temporarily restored office in Khaldiya. I was asked to wait outside while the group met. As I was called in, their greetings were abbreviated.

"Yacoub, we want you to join us as we open the university for the fall semester. We need you to teach. However, we think it would be better, under the circumstances in which you have placed yourself, for you assume a lesser role, at least for a time."

What did this mean?

"In other words, we will ask you to undertake your usual teaching duties, in the status of an adjunct, to be paid for each class and not as a full faculty member."

"So, you consider me to be important to the organization, in terms of what I do, but there are other factors."

"Exactly, there are other factors."

I agreed to their terms and went to find my old office, which was no longer usable. The books and files were gone, and there were cigarette butts and garbage around the room. I was consoled only by the fact that the other offices were mostly the same.

CHAPTER 38

The Kingdom of the White Camel

Diwaniyas began to meet again over the next month. In the evening as the weather warmed I saw gatherings of men in white disdashas outside in the gardens of the streetside villas. My regular group had convened, but I received no call. In the past I would not have considered an invitation unnecessary. But with the cold reception from every quarter, except Rabea, I was reluctant to impose myself. Rabea asked several times if I was going, but I ignored the question.

Divina and Rabea showed the kindness I did not receive elsewhere. I understood the source of their behavior but I couldn't bring myself to seek the basis for it.

I was done with religion. I had sought certainty in Islam, at first in an almost mathematical model, and failing that, I remained a Muslim who searched. When I reached the conclusion I had failed Islam, my search was done. What value could there be in a religion that made requirements without bestowing the ability to meet them?

I reluctantly began the process of reconstituting the Kuwait Tool and Electric. I went out to the home in Ahmadi on a day when the breeze carried the stench of the burning wells into the desert. Looters had destroyed most of the files. *This was for the best.* There was no longer a written record of what I did there.

The business was essentially defunct for the time. The burning oil wells were presently not the basis of a viable business plan. But the oil was still in the ground, and the money would flow out again. This fact was mathematical, more certain than Islam.

As I returned home, smelling of soot and burning oil, Rabea decided it was time to speak clearly about what she believed. Before I could change clothes and bathe, she asked me to sit and listen. Then, in great detail she said much of what I already knew, but there was more. She had read the Bible several times, and studied it in detail. She found the book to be one continuous, convincing story. Her exposure to other believers had occurred in a series: first Divina, then Lydia, and then Rebecca Freidecker. She knew (her use of this word surprised me, for how could she know) the Bible applied to her life and that the God described there had saved her. She had said this previously, but her saying it again was even more emphatic. "Yacoub, you need this message. You must read and discover for yourself. I love you and I want you to know as I know."

I was exhausted from the day and now from Rabea's words. I had a bad cough. I washed and went to sleep. In sleep the white camel visited and left me sweating after a prolonged visit. The sheets were soaked and Divina put them in the laundry.

It was time to return to the diwaniya of Abu Hassan. I drove over on Wednesday night, thinking it would be on the same day. The cars were lined up along the curb in front of the house. I went in the front door and into the hall and removed my sandals and entered the diwaniya.

The room fell silent for an awkward moment, abbreviated greetings were exchanged, and I took a seat on the cushion at the end of the row on the right. Although previously I would have been awarded a seat near the front, this was not the case after my self-imposed exile. Those who entered after me were afforded the usual privilege. A few of the group near me spoke. The evening waned as the conversation began to drift. Finally, there was a lapse in the flow, and I raised my voice in order to be heard by all. "I have a contribution for the diwaniya, a story that may entertain you." Abu Hassan, still the host of the diwaniya, frowned and signaled displeasure.

My story, foolishly chosen, dealt with the success of Islam during the Iraqi invasion. The story was dead on arrival. Soon the evening closed. I would not return to the diwaniya again.

I walked out into the night alone. The sky, which had formerly been clear, was now full of fine grains of sand. A toz was approaching, out of season. I got into my white Mercedes, covered with a thin layer of dust, and began the drive back to the house we were using. The story had not been in keeping with my role as a professor of the Sharia, or with the mood of the evening, and I was beginning to feel unwell. My old friend Dhuwahi struck a dissonant chord: "You don't even know your own heart, do you?"

Two weeks later Rabea summoned the courage. "Yacoub, perhaps we could go together to the church on the Gulf Road."

"It isn't safe for us. We can't go there together, and it's not safe for you to go alone."

Rabea knew I was right, but she had to make the request.

The next Sunday evening found us at the seaside by the Gulf Road. The evening was cool and dry with the wind off the Gulf. The water was beginning to clear, but still not enough for swimming. We saw the little carnival with the colored lights had reopened for business, and thinking the children might enjoy it, we proceeded down the beach. The rides were still filthy from the war and its dust and soot. A burned out Iraqi T-52 tank blocked part of the beach path, and we continued past. The tank was facing the sea from which the Iraqis had feared the attack would come. Soon we were in a more isolated area of the beach where the Gulf Road begins to turn away from the sea.

The cross of the National Evangelical Church was visible across the road. We would never go nearer. As we sat down to rest on a bench, there was a service in progress at the church. Rabea looked at me, but I couldn't face her.

The Filipino women's choir was singing, and the words of Luther's hymn, "From the Depths of Woe," beset me. My own woe was at its deepest ebb. The voices were high-pitched and clear, rendering them all the more penetrating. The phrase, "secret sins and misdeeds dark," pricked me deep; my own misdeeds were too dark to ever reveal, even to Rabea. And then the word "grace" attacked me. I rejected it. How could the phrase "grace alone availeth" apply to me? I had long ago exceeded the boundaries of any forgiveness.

The old hymn continued to its completion. But I had no response, and Rabea hid her tears.

"Rabea, there's nothing left for me. I heard the words of the hymn across the street. There's no possibility for me to be granted God's mercy. There is nothing more left for me to do. I must let go of everything but you."

"Yacoub, that's the point. And some time, even though I'm younger than you, you may have to let go of me. Most of life is about letting go. But you must learn there is more to all this than what you do for yourself, and there is more to know that you can always hold onto. Your name means one who grasps."

I was fifty-three. *What was left but the years?*

I slept that night with surprising ease. But about midnight, the dream, if it was a dream, began. I was transported, taken by some dream force, to a place I had been taken once as a boy. I found myself north of Wadi Al Batin, still full from the spring rains. My father had informed me the wadi was the remains of the Pishon River, one of the four rivers of Eden. In order to proceed back to bed, it would be necessary to cross the water.

In need of assistance, I looked for the white camel, who appeared from round a nearby dune. And then the shape of a man interposed himself in my path to the wadi. I couldn't distinguish the features of the man, but the only impression was of perfection of form and dress.

The white camel assumed a posture of aggression, one I had not previously observed. He lowered his head, extended his neck, and bared his teeth at the man by the water. The camel's black mole on his inner lip was visible again. And the jinn I had formerly denied was there, right in front of me. The white camel attacked the man with such force and violence that I feared the camel in a way I had never before experienced. I now saw the true character of the camel, like that of a demon, the camel I had followed for so many years.

Despite the camel's size, strength, and intent, he was no match for the man. He dispatched the camel, who retreated in fear back into the desert.

The man then turned his attention to me as I tried to cross the wadi, and we came together without the anger of the man's earlier encounter. But the man didn't allow me to progress. I couldn't retreat, and we grappled for what seemed like hours. As the contest continued, slowly it began to occur to me that the encounter and the wrestling match had a purpose beyond a dream. I recalled my Bibical namesake and his encounter at the ford of the Jabbok. Still, the match continued until I felt my back breaking. The pain was overwhelming.

When I awoke back in Ahmadi, I was unable to move due to the pain. Rabea bent over me. "Yacoub, you had a convulsion. Your back was arched and your head was thrown back. I don't know how long it lasted."

With help from the neighbors, Rabea was able to get me into the car, and then to a hospital near Ahmadi, where I was admitted. Three vertebrae were fractured. The electroencephalogram and CAT scan did not reveal the cause for the convulsion.

But I knew. I read again Genesis 32's account of my namesake's struggle with God. God cared enough for me that He presented an unmistakable vignette in the dream or vision. He was graceful beyond my conceiving of it. I finally knew what it meant to believe with the heart. And I knew I would not see the white camel again.

I related the dream, if it was a dream, to Rabea. She had already figured out most of the episode for herself, but upon hearing it from me, she wept and thanked God.

Of course, my trials were not done. That afternoon I received notice from Dr. Saternalia Allison that she was coming to Kuwait on sabbatical to assist with an archeological study on Failaka Island. She was invading my refuge.

The End

The Author

Jim Carroll is a medical school professor at Augusta University. Jim, along with his family of seven children (now eight) and wife, Shirley, resided in Kuwait for several years. He has traveled and written extensively about the Middle East. Jim and Shirley's memoir, *Faith in Crisis—How God Shows Up When You Need Him Most*, tells of their experiences during the Iraqi invasion of Kuwait in 1990. His book of short stories, *Diwaniya Stories*, is available on Amazon. His website and blog, www.allfaithsoil.com, discusses aspects of Middle East religion and politics.